COMING NEXT TIME...

STORIES! ARTICLES!
SHERLOCK HOLMES & DR. WATSON!

Sherlock Holmes Mystery Magazine #20
is just a few months away...watch for it!

Not a subscriber yet?
Send $59.95 for 6 issues (postage paid in the U.S.) to:

Wildside Press LLC
Attn: Subscription Dept.
9710 Traville Gateway Dr. #234
Rockville MD 20850

You can also subscribe online at
www.wildsidepress.com

FROM WATSON'S NOTEBOOK

For once, the only Sherlock Holmes adventure in this issue is my own recounting of that business in Boscombe Valley. Partly this is due to the increasing difficulty we are having in finding writers willing to work with my difficult-to-read notes of those cases yet to be told. (Please see Mr Kaye's comments below).

The second reason is that our next issue of *Sherlock Holmes Mystery Magazine* will be devoted entirely to my companion's exploits as what we both believe him to be, the world's first professional consulting detective.

Mr Holmes, as ever, is quite pleased at the prospect of an entire issue devoted to him. The tales to be offered in our next number include my own tale of the Stockbroker's Clerk, another case that I actually solved for Mrs Hudson and a third which, being a surprise, I'll not discuss. Other cases include one concening a British political candidate's election problems, the tale of a "wrong doctor," a strange story of a burnt song, a case involving Holmes's brother Mycroft and the story of what happened when a circus came to town with a distaff sharpshooter.

And now here is my colleague Mr Kaye....

–John H. Watson, M. D.

✗   ✗   ✗   ✗

As the good doctor stated above, this magazine is in need of more Holmesian pastiches, and while they do not have to be any of the tales yet to be told, that would be welcome, of course. In that wise, you will see below Dr W.'s cases that he never wrote up; to be precise, the only ones listed are ones that have not appeared in this magazine or in any of my three Sherlock Holmes anthologies.

Canonically Yours,
Marvin Kaye

✗   ✗   ✗   ✗

SHERLOCK HOLMES'S CASES STILL TO BE TOLD

- ADVENTURE OF THE TIRED CAPTAIN

- THE BISHOPSGATE JEWEL CASE (Inspector Jones will never forget how Holmes lectured the police force on it.)

- THE CAMBERWELL POISONING CASE (By winding up the dead man's watch, Holmes proved it had been wound up 2 hours ago, and that therefore the deceased had gone to bed within that time—a deed of the greatest importance in clearing up the case.)

- THE CASE OF THE DUKE OF HOLDERNESSE (Holmes claimed a reward.)

- THE CASE OF MME. MONTPENSIER

- THE CASE OF MR. FAIRDALE HOBBS

- THE CASE OF THE PAPERS OF EX-PRESIDENT MURILLO

- THE CONK-SINGLETON FORGERY CASE

- THE CUTTER ALICIA (Which sailed one spring morning into a small patch of mist from where she never again emerged, nor was anything further ever heard of herself and her crew… an unsolved case.)

- THE DRAMATIC ADVENTURE OF DR MOORE AGAR

- THE DREADFUL BUSINESS OF THE ABERNETTY FAMILY OF BALTIMORE

- THE DUNDAS SEPARATION CASE (One of the most revered names in England is besmirched by blackmail. "Only I can stop a desperate scandal.")

- THE FAMOUS SMITH-MORTIMER SUCCESSION CASE (1894)

- THE INTRICATE MATTER IN MARSEILLES

- THE NETHERLANDS SUMATRA CO. AND THE CO-LOSSAL SCHEMES OF BARON MAUPERTUIS (A case intimately connected with politics and finance and which led to Sherlock Holmes's near breakdown.) (Boer War?)

- THE PECULIAR PERSECUTION OF JOHN VINCENT HARDEN

- THE SHOCKING AFFAIR OF THE DUTCH STEAMSHIP FRIESLAND (Which so nearly cost us both our lives.)

- THE SINGULAR TRAGEDY OF THE ATKINSON BROTHERS AT TRINCOMALEE

- THE ST. PANCRAS CASE

- THE TANKERVILLE CLUB SCANDAL

- THE TRAGEDY OF WOODMAN'S LEE

- THE VENOMOUS LIZARD OR GILA ("Remarkable case, that!")

- VIGOR, THE HAMMERSMITH WONDER

ASK MRS HUDSON

by (Mrs) Martha Hudson

Dear Mrs Hudson,

I wonder which cases of Mr Holmes interested you the most?
Armand Cassenweiler

⚡ ⚡ ⚡

Dear Mr Cassenweiler,

There is only one and that is because I was involved. "His Last Bow" is one of the few stories not written by Dr Watson, for he was living elsewhere when it happened. Mr Holmes invited him to write it, but the good doctor declined, suggesting, instead, his literary agent, Arthur Conan Doyle (later knighted). The case concerned a spy, German, I think, though my memory is not quite as keen as it used to be. I am certain that it also involved Mr Holmes's brother Mycroft, but at a distance. Well, I am not acquainted with all of the details and Mr Holmes says that Mycroft prefers it that way.

There was one other similar case that called upon myself and Mr Holmes, but I can say little about it, for it was recorded by an American by the name of Manly Wade Wellman. Its title, I believe, is "The Man Who Was Not Dead," or something like that.

Sincerely,
Mrs (Martha) Hudson

⚡ ⚡ ⚡ ⚡

Dear Mrs Hudson,

May I inquire how well you know Dr Watson's agent Conan Doyle?
Lady Braxton

⚡ ⚡ ⚡

Dear Lady Braxton,

I am honoured to reply to your question regarding Dr Doyle! (Yes, he shares Dr Watson's profession—actually, both of them, for he is also an author, and a cracking good one, if I may say so.)

There are two aspects to my answer: the personal one, and the literary reply.

Personally, I have frequently gone out of my way to make resplendent dinners for Dr Doyle—more than I can remember!—and on these festive occasions, I have seen Mr Holmes eat ever so much more than he usually does, which is ever so seldom. Both doctors are accomplished story-tellers and they vie to better the other, but it always comes down to a draw each time. Dr Watson always regales us with Holmes tales he has not yet written up (sometimes Mr Holmes glowers at him, but he never tries to prevent him from continuing). Dr Doyle has told us many tales about a French military officer named Gérard, which pleases Mr Holmes, for Brigadier G, as he calls him, was one of his relatives. For that reason, Dr Doyle does not speak about Dr Edward Challenger, also related to Mr Holmes. It seems the professor's most famous adventure, in which he actually brought to London a *living* pterodactyl (!!!), intimately involved Mr Holmes, who adopted the disguise of Lord John Roxton (for details, consult our editor Mr Kaye's collection *The Game is Afoot*).

Concerning the literature by Dr Doyle that I have read—and enjoyed—there is his excellent semi-historical novel, *The White Company*. I've also perused with great interest two of the doctor's shorter works, *The Lost Special* and *The Man with the Watches*, but I never allude to either if Mr Holmes might hear, for he is anonymously involved in each case as a letter-writer to one or two (I forget) London newspapers. The problem is that in   at least one of these adventures, his theory, though plausible, was … I hesitate to say it … *wrong*.

Mrs (Martha) Hudson

✗   ✗   ✗   ✗

Dear Mrs Hudson,

I am a plain and simple bar-keep in Soho, but I am totally devoted to reading about Mr Holmes. I enjoy your columns very much, and especially revel over the recipes that you usually share with we readers; I have prepared several and have always relished the results!

My question concerns the fact that you often share main course recipes, and sometimes one involving vegetables; desserts, too.

But I have never seen any formulae for mixed drinks. Perhaps that is because Mr Holmes and Dr Watson prefer wine and beer?

A Whiskey Worshipper

✗   ✗   ✗

My Dear Whiskey Worshipper,

I am ever so glad that you asked this! It is true that both of my illustrious tenants favour various sorts of wine as well as ale, beer, bitters, lager, porter, stout, what-have-you. But I do confess that I like an occasional mixed drink. These were a bit uncommon in past years, but they became one of the best contributions that we were given by our neighbours, especially the Americans and the French.

In this issue of *Sherlock Holmes Mystery Magazine*, and in the next two such numbers, I shall confine myself to stronger alcoholic concoctions.

Yr Fellow Whiskey (and Whisky) Worshipper,

Mrs (Martha) Hudson

✗   ✗   ✗   ✗

Dear Mrs Hudson

I am afraid my question is indelicate—but I have heard rumours that Mr Holmes may be the father of that stupendously over-weight New York investigator Nero Wolfe.

Professor Jason Rickman, a genealogist

✗   ✗   ✗

Dear Professor,

I have been asked this before, but I chose to ignore such queries. But at last I got up the courage to ask Mr Holmes. He was, I am relieved to report, not at all offended. He merely laughed and shook his head. However, the look on Dr Watson's face showed deep disapproval. Therefore, when I could address him without his room-mate being aware of it, I tried to solicit an answer from him, but—albeit regretfully—he shook his head.

"Mrs H," said he, "I should like to oblige you, but I am constrained not to discuss this—"

"By Mr Holmes?!"

"Oh, no! Not at all! The difficulty stems from a New York City attorney who represents Mr Wolfe."

Well, my dear Professor Rickman, you see that I have no answer to give you. And I do regret it, if only for my own unjustifiable curiosity.

Mrs (Martha) Hudson

✗   ✗   ✗   ✗

Now, as promised, here are a few of the drink recipes that I personally like and sometimes serve to personal guests visiting me at Baker Street.

CONGRESSIONAL COCKTAIL

There are few mixed drinks that employ scotch, which generally does not mix well. But here is an exception to the rule.

2 jiggers of blended scotch (3 ounces)
1 ounce of dry vermouth
1 teaspoon of Absinthe (Pernod may be substituted)
1 lemon peel

1. Blend all three with ice and stir.
2. Place lemon peel into the drink.

✗   ✗   ✗   ✗

METALLIC TWIST

3 tablespoons of beef bouillon
1 ounce of Bombay gin
2 teaspoons of lemon juice
Worcestershire sauce, to taste
¼ teaspoon of salt
black pepper, to taste
2 droplets of Tabasco

1. Shake everything together.
2. Pour into a whisky glass.

✗   ✗   ✗   ✗

KILTED WONDER

1 teaspoon of Drambuie
1 teaspoon of vermouth
3 tablespoons of Polish vodka

1. Mix with ice.
2. Strain into a cocktail glass.

SCREEN OF THE CRIME

by Kim Newman

This month, I'm looking back at four films which share a title and highlighting several of the less-familiar screen incarnations of the Great Detective…

SHERLOCK HOLMES DIE GRAUE DAME (1937)

Though subtitled *Die Graue Dame* (*The Grey Lady*), this German film isn't a remake of the 1909 Danish film *Den Graa Dame* (*The Grey Lady*). The earlier movie, one of a Holmes series starring Viggo Larsen, was an adaptation of *The Hound of the Baskervilles* which substituted a lady ghost for the spectral dog. This is quite another thing, and diverges far more from the Doyle template than other German Holmes films of the period like the 1929 and 1937 movies called *Die Hund von Baskerville*.

Set in an elaborate if stagebound cosmopolitan London somewhere between the British whodunits published in green Penguin books and *telefono bianco* haut bourgeois melodramas of contemporary Italian cinema, this *Sherlock Holmes* offers pudgy, cheerful, cigar-smoking detective Jimmy Ward (Hermann Speelmans), who doesn't seem that much like Holmes, as a hero. Ward's manservant John (Werner Finck), who sneezes in the dark while they're waiting for a break-in and alarms the culprit, is even less like Watson. Then, late in the day, it turns out that Ward is Sherlock Holmes after all (as given away by the title), and he puts on a flat cap and takes up a pipe in a way which makes him resemble the sort of Holmes seen in German films (if not Paget illustrations).

A few neat moments (a rogue pretending to be dead in the street to distract a passing policeman and servants while a confederate slips in to rifle for those papers) are staged effectively, but it's mostly drawing room or nightclub conversations without even the atmospherics of most of the Edgar Wallace-derived *krimis*. There is a song, belted out in a smoky dive by Ursula Hercking in a mode somewhere between Dietrich and Weill (fishnets, body-stocking with a heart-shape torn out, shoulder bow). The plot involves stolen plans, shady sisters (blonde Trude Marlen, a goodie; dark Elisabeth Wendt, a baddie), poisoned cigarettes, that bit from "A Scandal in Bohemia" where a cry of "fire fire" drives a culprit to reveal their secret safe, Inspektor Brown of Scotland Yard (Ernst Karchow), Mabuse-like spymaster Barnov (Edwin Jurgensen), and coded-as-gay poodle lover Archibald Pepperkorn (Harry Lorenzen). Written by Hans Heuer and Erich Engels, from the Müller-Puzika play *Die Tat des Unbekannten*; directed by Engels, who also made two Crippen movies, *Dr Crippen en Bord* (1942) and *Dr Crippen Lebt* (1958).

✗   ✗   ✗   ✗

SHERLOCK HOLMES: THE STRANGE CASE OF MISS ALICE FAULKNER (1981)

A live performance of William Gillette's 1901 play, staged by the Williamstown Theatre Festival and recorded by HBO for broadcast in a series of taped music and theatre productions called *Standing Room Only*. Following Broadway success as *Dracula*, Frank Langella takes another Victorian leading role; Christopher Lee, Jeremy Brett (who took over from Langella on tour with *Dracula*), and Richard Roxburgh have also pulled off this double, incarnating the great good and evil Supermen of the 1890s as mirror images.

Though he might have been too louche and romantic for Conan Doyle's Holmes, Langella is well-cast as Gillette's... the actor-writer, fashioning the sleuth as a star part for himself, blended elements of "A Scandal in Bohemia," "The Final Problem," and other stories but shifted emphases to play up the witty banter and have the cerebral hero eventually discover his own emotions. At the end, Holmes does not sacrifice his life to rid the world of the evil Professor Moriarty (George Morfogen) but follows his triumph over his arch-enemy by abandoning his career for a new-found love interest.

In the 1922 John Barrymore silent version of the play, this seems ludicrous, but Gillette writes Holmes's realisation of the loneliness and coldness of his life with some subtlety. In the coda, Holmes trades on the gratitude heroine Alice Faulkner (Laurie Kennedy) feels to him for saving her life to manipulate her into handing over love letters that might wreck a Royal Engagement (written to her late sister, not her: Gillette couldn't have got away with making an immoral adventuress like Doyle's Irene Adler a heroine). Instantly, the detective is ashamed of his own brilliance and resolves to be a better man in a way that means giving up his profession. With audience reaction audible on the soundtrack (the throwaway "elementary, my dear Watson" gets a round of applause) and performances pitched to the back stalls, the thriller aspect doesn't really translate to television, but the back-and-forth exchanges of pointed insults are amusing and Langella expresses a delight in his own cleverness that's quite appealing.

Morfogen rolls his eyes and leers evilly as the Napoleon of Crime and Richard Woods blusters in the Nigel Bruce manner as a Dr Watson who has married and settled down, which means he has less to do but also serves as an example to his friend. Tom Atkins of *The Fog* and *Halloween III* does a creditable cockney thug accent as Moriarty's chief bruiser, Susan Clark (who had mixed with Holmes in *Murder By Decree*) is the femme fatale, Dwight Schultz of *The A-Team* is a shady character, familiar taffy-faced bit-player William Duell (the shoeshine boy informant in *Police Squad!*) is a butler, and a twelve-year-old Christian Slater takes the role of Billy the page. "Sebastian Moran" and "Hugo N. Furst" are listed in the credits as playing roles which turn out to be Holmes and Moriarty in traditionally terrible disguises. Produced for the stage by Peter H. Hunt (*1776*); directed for television by Gary Halvorson (*The Adventures of Elmo in Grouchland*).

✗　✗　✗　✗

SIR ARTHUR CONAN DOYLE'S
SHERLOCK HOLMES (2009)

This cheapskate, shot-in-Wales knock-off of the Guy Ritchie-Robert Downey Jr. film can't even be bothered to extend any originality on a title—would *Sherlock Holmes vs Spring-Heeled Jack* or *The Mystery of the Whitechapel Dinosaur* have used up too much letraset?—and so filmographies are now forever stuck with two 2009 films that go by *Sherlock Holmes*. It opens during the Blitz, with an aged Watson dictating one final memoir to a Miss Lucy Hudson (Rachael Evelyn) who, implausibly, has never heard of Sherlock Holmes. Equally implausibly, this is one of those "the world is not yet ready to know" cases—which implies that somehow Holmes managed to keep secret a business which winds up with a giant robot dragon laying waste to half of London and setting fire to the Houses of Parliament in 1882. The mystery proper begins with a giant squid wrecking a bullion ship in the English Channel, which prompts Inspector Lestrade (William Huw) to call in Holmes (Ben Syder), who makes a quick deductive diagnosis (acceptably Doylean) which wraps up an autopsy Watson (top-billed Gareth David-Lloyd, from *Torchwood*) is supposed to perform so the medical man can be available to assist the great detective.

As it happens, Watson's first job is pointlessly to dangle off a cliff—an incident which somehow tells him the gold is missing from the wreck he doesn't even see, and though he notices an apparent drowning man in the waves he fails to mention this when he's hauled to safety. Then, there's a dinosaur attack in Whitechapel, as a medium-sized CGI tyrannosaur chomps down on a bank clerk who's trying to pay for a sixpenny knee-trembler with threepence. The beast shows up in a nearby park and chases a fairly unintrepid Holmes-and-Watson through the undergrowth—rather, a camera runs after the fleeing actors to save on the very few effects shots. The case leads to a copper-wire factory, where the dinosaur attacks again (upstairs) and kills someone who was about to divulge useful information. A unique stone on the dead man leads our heroes to lonely Handsworth Castle, near where Holmes grew up ("that explains a lot," deadpans Watson). There, everything becomes clear and we get a crowded second half.

The villain, who is only called Spring-Heeled Jack in publicity and never so much as stands on tiptoes let alone leaps (which makes this a bust as the first Spring-Heeled Jack film since *The Curse of the Wraydons* in 1946), turns out to be Holmes's brother (Dominic Keating), a police inspector retired after being crippled on the job who blames Lestrade for accidentally shooting him in the back (he didn't) and has manufactured a range of Jules Verne gadgets to help him get revenge. The brother isn't Doyle's Mycroft but a new character named Thorpe Holmes, and his mechanical marvels include a steampunk Iron Man suit which means he can clump around and have fights despite being handicapped, the robot dinosaur and squid (no explanations for how he got them to the scenes of crimes unnoticed), a lady automaton (Elizabeth Arends) he intends to have crash Buckingham Palace as a suicide bomber, and two flying machines (the fake dragon and a combination hot air balloon/helicopter) the Holmes Brothers use to duel in the overambitious climax. All this is even more off-model than Guy Ritchie's Holmes, but considerably less entertaining—as in the same company's *MegaShark vs Giant Octopus* or *Snakes on a Train*, you get only the most half-hearted attempt at delivering on the promise of wild fantastical action.

Syder is much shorter than David-Lloyd, rarely advantageous in a Holmes, and is furthermore a reedy, floppy-haired, unimposing youth with a thin voice—he may give the worst Holmes performance in a seriously-intended talking picture to date (it's odd that the more physically suitable Keating didn't get the job). David-Lloyd, the first Welsh Watson since Dudley Moore, gets a bit more action to justify his billing—he wrestles the terminatrix bomb to the ground outside the Palace, though previously he'd taken a shine to her and invited her to the opera (though he has to cry off to go dinosaur-hunting). With the possible exception of Arends as a robot, no one makes much of an effort to be convincing or even interesting. Catriona McDonald is a hefty Mrs Hudson. As for the details, this is a rare film to put 221 on Holmes's front door—which makes sense—though Caernarvon can't really run to anything that looks remotely like Victorian Baker Street. In what might conceivably be a *Doctor Who* in-joke, it turns out that the hero's real name is Robert, but he uses his middle name because "no one would remember a detective called Robert Holmes." Written by Paul Bales (*The DaVinci Treasure*, *100 Million BC*, *MegaFault*), who might once have read a Sherlock Holmes story: he uses that beggar who pesters Watson but turns out to be the detective in disguise bit, but weirdly gives Holmes the Batman-like trait of never using a gun—except when forced to kill his brother to save his best friend—which doesn't square with the way the Hound of the Baskervilles was killed, for instance. Directed by Rachel Goldenberg (*Sunday School Musical*). Given that it's got Sherlock Holmes *and* dinosaurs, it really ought to be more fun.

✗   ✗   ✗   ✗

SHERLOCK HOLMES (2011)

George Anton is one of a new breed of essentially amateur film-maker, making no-budget, non-professional feature-length efforts which get posted to YouTube rather than given even a token commercial release. He is credited on *Sherlock Holmes* as director, producer, editor, cinematographer and composer—and I'd not be surprised to find out screenwriter "David Wallace" is a pseudonym. Anton's earlier *Dracula* (2009) uses very little of the novel and is mostly perhaps-autobiographical stuff about grubbing on the margins of the film industry, but this is a more focused effort and at least tells a proper story—because, as it admits in the end credits, it's a close adaptation of *The Woman in Green* (1945), a Basil Rathbone-Nigel Bruce Holmes film scripted by Bertram Milhauser.

The Woman in Green was one of the series of Universal films which brought the Great Detective into then-contemporary London. Though no locale is actually mentioned, Anton's *Sherlock Holmes* doesn't attempt to disguise its American locations (in Los Angeles and Florida) and includes a few cell-phones and contemporary references to establish that this is the present day. The police, represented by Inspector Gregson (Steve Acker), are baffled by a series of murders in which young women have fingers snipped off by a killer with a set of garden secateurs. Holmes (Kevin Glaser) is called in to investigate. While meeting Gregson in a bar, Holmes conveniently spots movie producer Fenwick (Gary Gansel) drinking with the purportedly glamorous Lydia (Kathy Shook)—the dialogue suggests she could be mistaken for her date's daughter, but she's a frankly mature and matronly femme fatale—and somehow tumbles that they're mixed up in the case. Expert hypnotist Lydia is in league with a loudly-dressed Moriarty (Daniel Rios): their racket is to dupe rich men into believing they are murderers by having them wake up after a date with the mesmerist to find severed fingers in their pockets and then blackmailing them. The plot plays out as it does in the 1945 film, but in drab, hotel-like settings and with any trace of action or excitement rigidly excluded.

Glaser's Holmes is short, chubby, and wears a flat cap (perhaps after the manner of those German Sherlocks of yore) while sucking on an unlit pipe. For some reason, Anton chooses to cut all Rathbone's deductions and witty remarks so this sleuth is a tiresome bore as well as a poor stand-in for Doyle's hero. Watson (Charles Simon) is a blithering idiot who gets lines like "there ought to be a law against fat people owning birds" and responds to an assassin disguised as a beggar with "oh bugger off—I'm on a mission of mercy." Poor as the leads are, they're often upstaged by walk-on players—like Ada Span as Mrs Hudson—who can barely get their lines out. Even Shook, the default leading lady, mangles her dialogue, referring to "childless tricks" when she means "childish tricks." The scene transitions are done with comic book pages that peculiarly run the action backwards.

If you're a Holmes completist or just curious—www.youtube.com/watch?v=0iad2dYsD7c. Anton has also made *Robinson Crusoe* (2008), *Apocalypse Now* (2012), *The Passions of Jesus Christ* (2012), *Aliens* (2013), *Dead on Arrival* (2013), *Romeo & Juliet* (2014), and *Men in Suits* (2015).

✗

Kim Newman is a prolific, award-winning English writer and editor, who also acts, is a film critic, and a London broadcaster. Of his many novels and stories, one of the most famous is *Anno Dracula*.

PODCASTING

CAN IT REPLACE THE SERIALS
OF THE '30'S AND '40'S?

by Lisa Cotoggio

A while back I moderated a panel for the Mystery Writers of America's New York Chapter Dinner. The topic was "Solving the Promotional Mystery."

Now while I thought that I had assembled an interesting group of publicists, marketers, and authors, who, I must say, gave an excellent overview of all authors can do to extend the sales and shelf-life of their books, the audience seemed to focus all their questions on one single point: Podcasts. Which, by the way, can be attributed to Jonathan Santlofer's keen insight on the subject.

Jonathan is podcasting his novel, *Anatomy of Fear* (*jonathansantlofer.com*) to what has become a hugely growing audience. He explained how he sets himself up in his writer space, which is located in an old furrier loft on the lower West Side of Manhattan and reads one chapter a week to his listeners, who just love the idea of not only being able to picture his characters come to life by the very author who scribed them, but also imagining the old furrier loft from which he does his esteemed work.

As an author, it made me ponder the thought: are we as authors missing out on a generation of readers whose maturity has impaired their eyesight? Though the answer to that question is quite obvious. We now, through the magical technology of Podcast, have the ability to change it in our favor. And why shouldn't we?

Looking back to the early days of my childhood, my father used to tell me of the nights he spent with his family gathered around the radio listening intently to every word of *The Shadow*, *The Lone Ranger*; and of course, *The War of the Worlds*, made infamous by the actual belief of an alien attack.

And while I belong to the tail end of the "*Babyboomer Generation*," the opening lines to those three shows still haunt the dark corners of my mind merely through memories of conversations with my father, born during the era known as the "*Silent Generation*":

Who knows what evil... lurks... in the heart of men? The Shadow knows!

A fiery horse with the speed of light, a cloud of dust and a hearty 'Hi-yo, Silver, away!' The Lone Ranger!

We interrupt this program to bring....

Riveting. Wouldn't you agree? Of course you would, which brings us back to our topic: Podcasting. A series of audio or video digital-media files which are distributed over the Internet by syndicated download through Web feeds to portable media players and personal computers. The radio of the future.

Wouldn't we all like to have that kind of gripping attention by a beloved audience of readers? Yes. And they on the same hand would love to have us read to them. The thought of being able to relive a fascinating part of one's childhood is a cherished moment, especially late in one's life.

✗

A top ten finalist in the 2002 Nevada Film Office 15th Annual Screenwriting Award, Lisa Cotoggio has worked as a script doctor for Summer Moon Productions and with Classical Alliance as a TV series creator and writer.

A BRETON HOMECOMING: CONCLUSION

by Peter James Quirk

(Note: When Part One ran in the previous issue, I was under the impression that this is a true story, but the author just
informed me that is really a work of fiction. I regret this misin-
formation, though it is still well worth reading.

–Marvin Kaye)

The story thus far…

It is the summer of 1940 during World War II, and the French
and British forces have been devastated by Nazi Germany's *Blitz-
krieg* tactics, although the majority of the British army plus many
thousand French soldiers were rescued by the British Royal Navy
from the beaches of Dunkirk and transported across the English
Channel. The remainder of the French Army, those who weren't
either killed or captured, struggled to make their way home. This
included many young men from the North-Western province of
Brittany, where the fisherman Yann Le Corr and his friend Padrig
anxiously awaited news of Yann's son (also named Yann). Eventually they learned that Yann was wounded and under the care of a
doctor in Nantes, a large city in the Loire Estuary. They resolve
to go there in their fishing boat and bring him home. As the story
continues, the two fishermen have just arrived in Nantes.

2 (CONTINUED)

At that moment, the roar of an engine brought us to our feet.
And as our eyes scoured the waterfront, a motorcycle and sidecar
turned onto the dock from between two abandoned warehouses. It
roared up to the jetty, and the soldier astride the machine, a splen-
didly attired cavalryman replete with helmet, jodhpurs, and black-
leather gaiters, dismounted and unclipped a sub-machine gun from
beneath the handlebars. He held it loosely but kept it aimed in

our general direction as the man in the sidecar, a ranking officer, stepped out and pulled himself erect beside him.

"Don't do or say anything stupid," I warned my volatile companion. "Our story is plausible. I just need to stay alive long enough to tell it."

At that moment, the officer, a major, called out in fluent French: "Step down from the boat and put your hands on your heads. Then walk toward us slowly."

As we climbed down to the dock and my back was turned to the Nazis, I whispered nervously to my companion: "Be really careful, Yann. The officer speaks very good French."

"Where are you from and what is your business?" demanded the major as he approached.

We stopped momentarily, and I somehow shook off my funk as though it were stage fright, and I was back at the *auberge* in front of an audience preparing to tell one of my famous tales of Breton peasant life:

"We are Breton fishermen, *Herr Major*," I said, lowering my hands slowly. "We sail out of Kérity, which lies north-west of Nantes, near the Pointe de Penmarche."

"Ahh, yes," he interjected, "that's Bigouden country, is it not? I know that region rather well. I used to spend summers with a family near Quimper when I was a student."

My face must have telegraphed my amazement, because he laughed out loud as he continued:

"You're a long way from home. What brings you to Nantes?"

"*Herr Major*, one of our crew was badly hurt in an accident at sea. We brought him to Nantes and left him with a doctor. Now we have come to take him home."

His eyes narrowed as he pondered our circumstance. Then he ordered his man to lower his weapon. "We in the National Socialist High Command," he said, as he reverted to French and his demeanor moderated from menacing to merely pompous, "are acutely aware of the injustices inflicted on the Breton peoples by the archaic feudal covenant still enforced by the local *seigneurs* and condoned, nay, encouraged by the elitist central government."

He paused to gauge the effect his pontificating had on us, and then he looked at Yann as though expecting a response, which was clearly dangerous.

"Alas, *mein Herr*," I interjected, "we are fishermen, and although we work long, hard hours, we are mostly self-employed; so we are not really affected by the same struggles as farm workers."

"Well," he continued. "You will find that the German occupying forces, ably supported by your loyal Vichy government, will improve the lot of both the land workers and the fishermen of Brittany. Tell me, is your friend able to walk? If not, perhaps I can arrange a vehicle to bring him down to the quay."

"P-please," I stammered, alarmed for a moment that he might be sincere, "don't trouble yourself. I'm sure we'll manage just fine." I paused, grasping for subterfuge. "I believe the doctor has a car," I added hastily.

"Very well," he said, pulling a notebook and pen from his pocket and scribbling something down. "Here, take this; this will serve as a safe-conduct through the town. That is my name at the top. Don't hesitate to try to find me if you encounter difficulties."

"Thank you, *Herr Major*," I said, incredulously, as I stared down at this unanticipated bounty. Yann, who apparently realized that the scales were tipping slightly in our direction, nudged me in the ribs:

"Ask him about the *Kenavo*," he said, ever the practical seaman.

"And our boat, *Herr Major*?" I asked. "My captain wishes to know if we can leave it here safely while we pick up our shipmate."

"*Bien sûr!*" he replied, taking back our precious pass and adjoining a hasty postscript. He handed it back with a flourish. "This gives you three days, my Breton compatriot. That should be more than enough time." With that, he clicked his heels, threw his right arm in the air and rendered the obligatory: "*Heil Hitler!*" Then the two men clambered back onto their machine and disappeared back between the same two buildings.

Yann shook his head in disbelief. "Did he say what I thought he said?"

"He did," I affirmed. "According to him, the only reason the Nazis came to Brittany is to help the Breton peasants overthrow their French oppressors. But whatever—as long as we have this pass, we can come and go as we please."

Yann nodded, then stepped forward with a satisfied smirk and spat on the ground where the German Major had stood just moments before.

We battened down and lashed a tarpaulin over the *Kenavo* and ventured into the town. This once proud capital of Brittany had been in German hands for just two weeks, and disbelief and even shame were palpable on the faces of the people as they hurried through the streets with heads down and eyes averted.

We found our doctor's house—a three-level Victorian with roof turret and brick façade—just as the shadows of early evening began stretching into twilight. And when we tapped lightly on the heavy oak door, a woman's voice, more suspicious than nervous, called from within: "Who are you and what do you want?"

"We are Breton fishermen, and we're here in search of a shipmate. We were told that Doctor Bertrand might be able to help us."

"Just a minute," came the response, and we heard footsteps, retreating—fading. Moments later, different steps—heavier, slower—returned, and then a man's voice called out from behind the door:

"This friend of yours, does he have a name?"

The moment I responded, the door cracked open and a balding, middle-aged man with a heavy moustache peered out into the gloom. "What makes you think your friend is here?" he asked, as his eyes darted nervously up and down the street.

"We were given this address by one of his army comrades," I explained. "This is his father, and I am Padrig Le Bras, an old shipmate and friend. We are here to bring him home. Your patient will vouch for us."

With that the doctor relaxed, and he opened the door wider and stepped aside: "Come in quickly, both of you. The curfew goes into effect soon, and they arrest people who venture on the street at night."

He ushered us into his surgical waiting room. "Please, gentlemen, sit. It must have been a difficult journey." He turned then to Yann: "Did you come by train, Mr. Le Corr?"

"Mr. Le Corr speaks very little French," I interjected. "Do you speak Breton?"

The doctor shook his head apologetically. "No, I'm afraid not. But this is unfortunate; I have bad news, and I would rather disclose it personally."

My heart sank. "Oh God! No. He's not dead?"

"Your friend has been through hell these last few weeks," he replied. "But, no. He's not dead. But—and I'm very sorry to have to tell you this—last week we had to amputate his left leg at the knee. It couldn't be avoided; gangrene was setting in."

I glanced at my companion, but he had not followed the conversation. But when I translated the appalling news, his head slowly sank into his hands and he turned away in despair.

Doctor Bertrand continued: "Your friend is hidden upstairs under the mansard. Come, I will show you the way."

I tried to put my arm around Yann's shoulders, but he shook it off roughly as we followed the doctor up the main stairs to a landing overlooking the foyer. He pointed to a huge ornamental washstand that stood against the wall.

"If you lift that to one side," he said, "you will find a detachable panel which conceals a stairway to the attic. The stairs will take you to your son." He pulled a watch from his vest pocket and snapped open the top. "You may go up and see him now. But be careful. He will probably be asleep, and he keeps a service revolver under his pillow. If you startle him he may try to shoot you."

As soon as we removed the panel, Yann called up to his son in Breton and followed his voice up the stairs. The doctor and I lingered on the landing to give them a few moments alone. There was a short, uncomfortable silence, and then we both began speaking simultaneously. The doctor held up his hands: "I'm sorry," he said. "What were you going to say?"

"Do you think he is fit to travel?" I repeated.

"That's a difficult question to answer," he replied. "In a perfect world, of course, I'd have to say no—especially not on a tiny fishing boat. But under these circumstances, I don't think we have much of a choice. There will never be a better opportunity to return him to his home and family."

I agreed with that assessment—we had a pass to get us through the town; the boat was ready to sail, and I knew that Yann would never leave without his son. So we began discussing any difficulties we might encounter. And while we stood there on the landing, a tall woman, her iron-gray hair swept back into a chignon, ascended the stairs with a tray of bandages. She and the doctor exchanged smiles and he placed his arm around her shoulders when she stepped onto the landing:

"This is Nicole—my wife, my nurse, and my right hand. She has been taking care of your friend, and I see it's time to change his dressings."

We exchanged greetings, and then she slipped into the narrow stair well. The good doctor waved me in behind her, and the winding stairs brought me to a box room tucked directly beneath the slate and lath of the roof. I admit I had not known what to expect when I stepped into the room, but when I saw the figure lying on the floor in that cramped and dusty space, I scarcely recognized my young friend.

Gone was the sturdy, self-reliant young man I had sailed beside for more than a dozen years; in his place was a defeated soldier with haggard features and sunken eyes that were accentuated by shadows thrown from an oil lamp on the floor beside the mattress. I knelt beside him and took his hand, and was rewarded by a wan smile:

"Padrig, Padrig," he said weakly, "I feared I would never see you again."

I glanced up at his father as I struggled to find words to reflect my sorrow at his plight while, at the same time, offering some solace. And I realized that, in his devastation, Old Yann had also been unable to comfort his son sufficiently. I turned back to the boy, put my arms around him and kissed his cheeks. But in the end all I could manage was a weak, "Thank God you're alive," and I lowered my eyes in shame.

Mercifully, the doctor's wife set her tray down beside me and began preparations for changing the dressings. So I pulled myself to my feet, took Old Yann by the arm and pulled him gently to one side.

"At least we have him back," I whispered. He nodded grimly, but there was no joy in those eyes.

During the next few days, I came to realize that my old friend was having great difficulty coming to terms with two inescapable facts: the sudden collapse of the invincible French army, after his comrades and he had struggled for four years in the trenches of the Great War; and the loss of his boy in terms of a shipmate and fellow fisherman. In the Brittany of the thirties and forties to lose one's only son's wage earning capacities was a calamity, but to have to nurse and financially support an amputee in addition was a devastating burden.

On the third day, we loaded Young Yann into the doctor's Citroën CV and brought him down to the river where the *Kenavo* chafed at her moorings, eager to carry him home. And because his patient was still weak from his surgery, the good doctor helped us carry him on board and make him comfortable on a field cot of fishing nets. Doctor Bertrand then cast off our lines and wished us God speed as we fired up our motor and pushed out into the Loire to begin our return voyage.

And as we island-hopped our way back up the coast, our passenger spent most of the first day in a drug-induced sleep. But by the second afternoon the salt air and the gentle roll of the ocean seemed to be having a healthful impact, so I sat him up in the stern, made him comfortable by propping up his stump with my duffel bag, and offered him the helm:

"Here," I said, with a wink. "If you can't pay your passage, you are going to have to work for it."

His contented expression told me all I needed to know as he grasped the tiller and ran a practiced eye over the trim of the sail. Then he looked off to the south-west over the vast expanse of the Atlantic Ocean and filled his lungs with air laced with the salt and spray of a thousand waves: "This is where the Good Lord intended me to spend my days, Padrig," he said. "And that's exactly what I intend to do from this moment on."

It was good to see Young Yann in such a positive frame of mind after all he'd been through, and we bantered back and forth, just as we had when he was a boy. And when he asked how we came to find him, I entertained him with a lighthearted version of our preparations and our outbound voyage, making sure to emphasize his father's critical role.

"But you," I said, when I had finished. "How did you end up in Nantes, of all places?"

"That's a long and twisted tale," he replied. "And I don't have anything like your story-telling skills. But if you'll bear with me, I'll do my best:

The regiment is stationed on the Maginot Line—on the edge of the Ardennes—two leagues from the Belgian border. We are bivouacked under canvas and they put us to work digging trenches. All day we are digging trenches—a maze of stupid trenches. In the evenings we sit around in our tents playing cards, drinking cheap wine and reminiscing about our homes, our families, and our former lives. This doesn't make us feel better, but it does remind us why we are here.

When our captains decide the trenches are ready, High Command comes down to inspect them. There are meetings at Battalion headquarters with parades and inspections—all the usual bullshit. First they make us dig through a mountain of mud, and then they expect us to get all cleaned up for inspection. I tell you, Padrig, the military has some stupid ideas about how to win a war.

But after all that, it turns out they don't like our trenches, or our position for that matter. The official word is we are too vulnerable. So they pull us back to the next hill and we start over. They pull this shit three times—it's like they want us to dig a fucking trench all the way back to Paris. But for me, the worst part is the planes. All the time we're digging, enemy spy planes fly over us, watching us—it's eerie. But does anyone try to shoot them down or chase them off? *Nann!* That would be too easy.

Then it begins! Suddenly, there are no more spy planes. Now the air is filled with *Stukas* raking our positions with machine-gun fire. Then their artillery starts—the sky is black with shells and mortars. The bombardment lasts for two days—we just sit in our trenches with our heads down. On the second day the regimental headquarters takes a direct hit, killing our colonel and his second-in-command.

When we hear about that, my sergeant says that's the end of us as a fighting machine. He says they were the only officers we had who knew what they were doing. According to him the rest of the staff officers got their commissions from political pandering—whatever that means; and our field officers, he says, are a joke—just kids—wet behind the ears.

On the third day comes the big push—wave upon wave of tanks, with infantry battalions moving in behind them. We try to hold 'em off, but it's like trying to hold back the tide—men are dying all around me. But it's the noise that really wears us down. The crash of guns; the screams of the wounded—you can't hear yourself think.

The sergeant receives word from field HQ: "Begin withdrawing your men in an orderly fashion!" Who do they think they're kidding? There's nothing orderly about being in Hell. Some men throw down their rifles and start running. When I see that, I want to run too—I'm just as scared as they are—but I'm in the same trench as the sergeant. But when he climbs out of the hole to try to stop the stampede, he's cut to pieces by machine-gun fire and his body falls back in the trench on top of me.

That's it. I'm out of there. We're all out of there. I heave his body to one side, scramble out of the hole and start running. I tell you, Padrig, I never ran so far or so fast in my life. But when the cannon roar fades and the carnage is far behind, I collapse on the outskirts of a forest hamlet and lie on the ground gasping for air. Some fifteen minutes later, when my body stops heaving and I pull myself to my feet, I discover to my shame and chagrin that my face and coat are covered with my sergeant's blood.

There's another soldier from my regiment skulking in the woods nearby, and together we head into the village, slinking between the houses like a couple of thieves. And beside the square, another man I know calls to me from one of the houses. Now there are three of us in this bombed-out settlement not knowing what to do or where to go.

Then the shelling starts afresh and the soldier from the house leads us back inside, and we take cover in the cellar. And for the first time that week I begin to feel safe—the rock walls are dense and substantial. But we're all exhausted, so we agree to stay there and rest up until dark and then try to make our way back to our lines—wherever the hell they are.

There we are, three Breton peasants sitting in the cellar of a house in an abandoned village in the middle of the Ardenne forest. Shells are flying overhead, and we have no idea where the Germans are, where the French are, or where we are. I am sitting on the floor with my back against a stone wall. Sitting beside me is Joseph Le Bris, a farm laborer from the Black Mountains.

Across from us is Marcel Guillou, a miller's son from Malestroit, on the Lanvaux Heath, north-east of Vannes. He is the first among us to shake off his fear, and he is soon restless, getting to his feet and poking around, testing the doors and peering into the cabinets.

"Aha!" he says, as he holds up a key, seemingly oblivious to the inferno outside. "This is more like it." He returns to the only locked door, swings it open and disappears inside.

Joseph turns a contorted and frightened face toward me: "What?" says he.

"Search me," I say, shrugging my shoulders. But our eyes are on the doorway. Where has he gone? What is he doing?

Marcel reappears with three bottles under his arm. "This'll make the day go better," he says.

We are suddenly very thirsty, and we jump to our feet.

"Is it cider?" asks Joseph, doubtfully.

"No. They don't make cider around here," says Marcel. "It's wine, red wine!"

He passes out the bottles, and I seize mine and pick at the cork with my bayonet. It refuses to budge. I jab at it but only succeed in stabbing my fingers. Frustrated, I shove the damn thing down into the bottle. At last it is mine. My lone victory in this crazy war. I hold my captive up by its neck:

"May Hitler rot in Hell," I say. "*Ar Breizh*!" I'm not being patriotic; I am railing at a God that allows the blind ambition of a fascist lunatic to put the world at peril.

"*Ar Breizh*," they echo, and we take long pulls at our bottles, none of us knowing whether we will ever see our homeland again.

The wine is rich and dry. It rolls down my throat and through my body, embracing and warming me as it passes, numbing my senses. The hell outside begins to fade as I wipe my mouth with the back of my hand and stumble against the wall. Marcel is standing in the middle of the room, savoring a mouthful. But it is Joseph, shell-shocked and frightened Joseph, who captures the moment. He is sitting back on the floor leaning against the wall and gazing reverently at his bottle:

"Jesus!" he says. "That'll settle your fucking nerves."

We say nothing more until our bottles are empty. By this time I am back on the floor next to Joseph, and we are both watching Marcel, who is rocking gently back and forth with his eyes closed. Then another shell lands, just missing the house, but the impact throws him to the ground. He picks himself back up, curses the air, and hurls his flagon at the wall.

"Those Nazi pigs," he says indignantly. "Don't they know it's the cocktail hour?" He dusts himself off. "Shall we have another?" he asks, as an impish grin lights up his war-torn and filthy face.

This seems like a good idea to me, but Joseph is not so sure: "I don't know, Marcel," he cautions. "We don't want to get drunk."

"Why the hell not?" says Marcel. "We could be dead any moment. Let's go out with a bang. Tell him, Yann."

"Just one more bottle, Joseph," I say. "It will keep our spirits up while we wait for it to get dark. Don't worry, my friend. We won't leave you down here."

Marcel chuckles at that and dives back into the stock. He returns with three more bottles.

"Here," he says, affecting a French accent. "Try a thirty-eight; one of my better years."

There's no mercy for the cork this time when I grasp my bayonet, and I drive it straight down into the bottle and take a quick swig. Meanwhile Marcel has pitched one to Joseph, but it slips between his fingers and drops to the floor, exploding at his feet.

"Damn!" he says. And he stares down at the puddle of wine as though it were his own blood.

"After all the crap we've been through today, that's nothing— nothing!" says Marcel. "There's plenty more where that came from. Here, catch this." He tosses over the other bottle and dives back into the stock room. Soon bottles come rolling out along the floor.

"Help yourselves, boys," his voice calls from deep within the cellar, just before another shell hits the house next door.

I don't remember how long we were down there, because I must have fallen asleep. But the next thing I know, a boot is kicking me in the ribs.

"*Raus, raus!*" I hear. I open my eyes and find myself staring straight down the barrel of a rifle.

"On your feet! *Hände hoch! Raus, raus!*" Teutonic roars fill the room.

I look around me. Marcel is on his feet with his hands in the air, and Joseph is picking himself off his knees.

They take us outside and herd us with some other prisoners in the village square. We stand there with hands on our heads while they search the rest of the buildings. Then they lock us in the village hall for the night. And as darkness falls on our makeshift prison the cannons of Hell go strangely silent.

There are about twenty prisoners in the hall, but only five of us are from Brittany. We group together in the back of the room. And as usual, Marcel is nosing around behind a platform. When he comes back, he has news:

"There's a way out of here," he says. "And the forest is just beyond the building."

Joseph and I are ready to follow him anywhere. If he can pull wine out of the air, he can get us out of this. "Fine," I say. "Anything's better than a German prison camp."

"What about them?" says Joseph, jerking his thumb toward the other men standing around in small groups, talking in low tones.

"To hell with them," says Marcel. "Besides, we don't speak French. How can we tell them without alerting the *Boches*?"

"I don't know, but we can't just vanish." I am torn. Leaving them behind doesn't seem very patriotic, but I know we would have more chance of success on our own. "I can speak a few words," I offer. "There's an officer over there. Why don't I tell him?"

I go to the officer, a captain of artillery, and ask him if he wants to try to escape, although I don't tell him how. But he's afraid the Germans will shoot him if someone tries it. I shrug and go back to the Breton group.

"We're on our own," I say. "He has cold feet."

"Okay," says Marcel. "Let's wait till everyone's asleep."

We all get down on the floor and pretend to settle in for the night. I actually do try to sleep, but my nerves are all jangled up from the fighting, the running, and the wine. Finally, Marcel whispers in my ear:

"Okay," he says. "It's time to get the hell out of here."

One by one, five Bretons sneak under the platform and climb up and out through a coal shoot. We find ourselves in a small enclosure at the back of the hall. There are no guards to be seen, and there are no lights except for a half moon that is diving in and out behind some wind-swept clouds. We wait for a minute, but there is no sound, and Marcel waves us on and leads us single file down a long alleyway to the edge of the sheltering forest.

We walk all night hoping we are going in the right direction. Finally, just as day breaks we come to the banks of a river. We follow the river away from the morning sun, towards the west, and eventually we come to a bridge guarded by a German patrol.

"Now what the hell do we do?" growls Joseph.

"Let's go back upstream and swim across," I offer.

But it turns out that swimming is not an option for Breton peasants. So we contemplate fighting our way across, but we don't even have our bayonets. Marcel, who has become our leader, decides to take a closer look, and he motions me to follow him.

"You men wait here," he says.

We creep up close to the road and onto a wooded knoll that affords us a view of the bridge. There are two guards at each end, and on our side there's a light truck parked alongside the road.

Marcel studies the scene for a moment, and his eyes light up:

"Okay!" he says. "The key here is to get down to that truck without being noticed. Stay here and keep an eye on them. I'm going to get the others."

I take a closer look at the truck and see what got him excited: There are rifles stacked in the back.

I nod and turn back to the bridge while my companion crawls back the way we came. While I am watching, one of the guards at our end sees something in the river and calls his companion over. Soon they are both leaning over the rail, completely distracted. I know there will never be a more opportune moment, but Marcel and the others are nowhere to be seen.

I don't know what comes over me, Padrig. I never before had the urge to be a hero. But before I know it I am creeping down the knoll to the back of the truck. I pull out a rifle. So far, so good, but from there I can no longer see the guards. I glance back at the knoll and see Marcel and Joseph peering down and motioning to me to stay still.

Suddenly Marcel jumps out and shouts: "Go, go!" And my four companions start running down from the knoll screaming their heads off. I spin out from behind the truck, drop to one knee and lift the rifle to my shoulder. I shoot one guard in the chest as he turns toward me, but the other one runs across the road and puts the truck between us.

I jump to my feet as I feed another shell into the chamber. I run around the truck and suddenly we're face to face. We both have our rifles at the ready. It's now or never! I fire at him, point-blank. I feel a sledgehammer blow to my leg, and I buckle and pitch forward onto the road.

I don't know how long I am lying there, but I hear shouts and gunfire from the other end of the bridge, and the sound of a motor turning over. Then I hear Marcel's voice and I feel myself being lifted into the truck. Then we are racing over the bridge with Joseph and Marcel blazing away like a couple of gangsters. We make it across, I remember, but after that things get hazy. Marcel tells me later I pass out from the pain.

I know I spend a lot of time lying in the back of that truck, and I vaguely remember being told we're in the Loire Valley. Then I am moved to a French truck and the following day to a car. The next thing I know we're riding through the streets of Nantes. Joseph and Marcel are still with me; they tell me the rest:

"When we get down to the truck," says Marcel, "we grab the two remaining rifles from the back and run to back you up. But we arrive just in time to watch you shoot it out with the German guards. You killed them both—great job. Meanwhile one of the other men cranks up the truck, and we put you in the back and head over the bridge as fast as we can go."

Joseph picks up the story: "Then we hook up with a French convoy that is heading for the Loire Valley to make a stand. The other two men are placed in infantry units, but they send us back with you to seek medical aid. Eventually we meet up with Doctor Bertrand who brings us back to his surgery in Nantes."

"We hear on the radio that Pétain has sued for an armistice, and Marcel decides to head home before the Germans move in. They promise to find my father when they get back. I guess you know the rest."

When Young Yann finished his narrative, he searched his father's eyes for the slightest sign of encouragement or perhaps even sympathy, but if he expected any, he was surely disappointed. Old Yann grunted, got to his feet and began adjusting the sail.

But then he turned to me, and I was looking into the eyes of a young man who had seen so much in so short a time. He had been a player on the world's stage for just a millisecond and had paid dearly for that privilege. What could I say to him? What words were there to comfort him? For the rest of his life he would struggle just to move around. Perhaps he could still fish for a living, but it wouldn't be easy.

Young Yann had been born into a world of poverty where his only asset was his healthy body and youthful vigor. And now that had been taken from him. I reached over and put an arm around his shoulder and gave him a squeeze. But even I, Padrig the storyteller, had no words of comfort for my friend. There was nothing I could think of to say that would have even an ounce of truth. So I sat there in the stern of our tiny boat, forlornly clutching his shoulders as the huge swells rolled in off the ocean systematically picking us up and letting us gently back down.

The following afternoon, we dropped anchor in Kérity harbor.

✗

Peter James Quirk is an author, freelance writer and outdoorsman who spends his winters skiing and snowboarding and his summers hiking, biking and playing tennis. His novel *Trail of Vengeance* has a strong ski theme; indeed, the villain of the story is a disgraced ski instructor. Many of his stories, however, cover World War II and its aftermath. It is a fascinating if tragic period to explore, and the villains and heroes are so easy to find.

THE PERFESSER AND THE KID

by Roberta Rogow

Hi, fellas! Glad to see the gentlemen of the Press are all here. And that you have time for a washed-up old pol like me. Especially with so many other bigwigs around. Fiorello gave a good eulogy, he's always good with words, and there were the usual eggheads who come out when one of their own goes. So, you're asking why I came out on a freezing cold day in January, just to sit in a church and listen to a lot of people talk about a man who did his best work nearly fifty years ago and hasn't been seen in public for the last fifteen.

See, I knew Dr. Tesla back in the old days on the Bowery and the East Side. In fact, if it wasn't for me, he wouldn't have lasted a day in New York.

You've all heard him tell it a thousand times. How he got robbed on the boat coming over, how he was left with four cents, how he walked to Edison's workshop, how he saw a man on the street with a piece of machinery, how he fixed it and got a buck for it, and how that was how he got the money to keep going until he could earn enough to rent a room. That's his story, and he's sticking to it.

But it's not the whole story! There was something else happened to him before he met the man with the machine and if you stand me to something warm, I'll tell it to you.

✗ ✗ ✗ ✗

You all know how I got my start, peddling newspapers and hustling on the streets. My old man needed the money, my mother, may she rest in Heaven, took it. Sure, I went to St. James's Catholic School, but as soon as class was out, I was on the streets with my papers looking for an opportunity to make another nickel.

One of the best places to hawk the papers was the plaza in front of Castle Garden, where the immigrants were coming in. These days they've got a fine facility on Ellis Island, but then it was

Castle Garden and it wasn't half so organized. The ships off-loaded, folks went in one side, come out the other, right into the hands of all kinds of grifters and touts, looking for easy marks, men who needed jobs, girls who might get hustled into something we don't want to talk about. And the first thing those immigrants wanted was a newspaper, assuming they could read it, and that's where us newsies came in. We were out there, waving out papers, yelling "Extra!" and getting as much attention as we could, not only from the greenhorns, but from the touts and grifters. I wasn't the biggest newsie there, but I was the loudest and I could spot the greenhorns who looked like they could read, so I did all right.

So I was peddling my papers and along came this feller, a long drink of water in a black coat and tie and a soft hat, what they call a Homburg, not a derby or a cloth cap, and I spotted him for a good mark for my papers so I ran up and yelled, "Getcha Post, Mister?"

He stopped and gave me the eye. "I regret that I only have four American pennies," he said, real precise, like a teacher.

"Paper only costs two cents," I said.

"I must go to the offices of the Edison Company," he said. "Can you instruct me how to walk there?" He spoke English, but very precise and with an accent I couldn't place. I tagged him as some kind of teacher so I called him the Perfesser in my mind.

"Come with me," I said. I don't know why, because I could have stayed right where I was and made a few more sales, but I led him away from the touts and grifters and into the streets of Manhattan. I guess even then I was the kind of guy who wanted to help people and this greenhorn sure needed help!

Once you got away from Castle Garden the streets were a crazy mess. Bob Moses has made a lot of changes, cutting through the alleys and side streets, putting in traffic lights, sticking signs all over the place, but back then there were no maps or signs and the garbage was piled waist high and there were no lights or cops directing traffic so it was all horses and they went every which way. I knew my way around, so I headed uptown to where the Edison company was located.

How'd I know where it was? Everyone knew about Edison and his electric lights and how he was hooked up with J.P. Morgan to put the electric lights into all the mansions on Fifth Avenue. Electricity was for the mucky-mucks, not for everyone else. It was the Perfesser who saw that changed, and I was a part of that, too. But that was a lot later. Then, it was gaslight on the streets, when there was a light at all.

The Perfesser set out, marching through the crowds like they weren't there, ignoring the bums and the peddlers and the easy women, eyes straight ahead. I ran to keep up with him. His legs were twice the size of mine and he didn't slow down to accommodate me. We went up Broadway to the Bowery and there he stopped short, so I nearly bumped into him.

We were right in front of Sharkey's, which was one of the most famous saloons on the Bowery. There were worse places, real dives, but Sharkey's was where the sporting crowd hung out, boxers and pool hustlers and gamblers, real hard men. The young sports from Uptown would come to Sharkey's slumming after they'd put in their time at fancy balls and dinners. No women, of course, not even the fancy ladies; Sharkey's was strictly stag.

The Perfesser didn't even look at the saloon. Right next to the swinging doors was a big sign: Billiards, and a staircase that led upstairs to Sharkey's second floor where the pool tables and poker players were.

The Perfesser spelled it out. "Billiards? I know billiards."

And in he went, up the stairs to the pool-room on the second floor where Sharkey and his boys were hanging out, waiting for a sucker to come along. And here he came in his long black coat and his foreign hat with his stringy mustache and his deep-set eyes. And me tagging along behind in knee pants because I was eleven years old and those days you didn't get long pants till you hit thirteen.

Did I know what I was doing? A kid in a pool hall? Sure, I knew I wasn't supposed to be anywhere near a place like Sharkey's. My mother would have cried, my old man would have my hide, but I couldn't help myself. I had to follow the Perfesser to see what would happen.

The Perfesser marches into the upstairs room at Sharkey's and says, "I wish to play billiards."

Every one of those Bowery characters stopped what he was doing and stared at this greenhorn with his funny way of talking and his fancy clothes.

Sharkey himself was sitting there in a big leather chair presiding in form. He was a big man and he filled up that chair like the King of the Bowery. He looked the Perfesser over and said, "The game here is Kelly pool."

"I do not know this Kelly Pool," said the Perfesser. "But the theory is the same, yes?"

He walked over to the pool table where the balls were still spread out from the last game. He picked up a cue and pointed it at one of the balls.

"The sphere is set into motion by the end of this rod. The vector depends on the angle of impact, the rate of impact and the quality of the cloth, yes?" He hefted the cue and eyed the balls. "The spheres are slightly smaller than the ones with which I am familiar, but the theory is the same."

I don't think any of those bums ever thought much about exactly what they were doing when they shot pool, but when you do think about it, I guess that's what pool is, sending the spheres in motion and betting on where they're going to wind up.

"Five cents a ball," says Mousey, who is Sharkey's assistant. He knew what was important and it wasn't the theory of shooting pool, it was the money you make from it.

The Perfesser's face fell. He only had the four cents.

I stepped up and said, "Here's the extra penny, sir." I added the 'sir' to be polite, to show that I knew how to address a real perfesser.

The Perfesser takes my penny and adds it to his four.

"I shall play for double or nothing," he announces. "I will take one shot. If I put the ball into the correct pocket, I will double my money. If I do not, I will lose."

Mousey looked over at Sharkey as if to ask, Is this gink legit?

Sharkey gave him the nod. "Go ahead, rack 'em up," he said. I guess it must have been a slow day, and he was ready for a little amusement. "A nickel to a dime you don't make the shot."

"A billiard ball is round," he says, "therefore the vector should be obvious. I shall use the cue ball to place the first one in the side pocket." And he did.

So now there was a nickel and five pennies on the pool table rail.

"Double or nothing," said the Perfesser, and Sharkey nodded again.

And so it goes, one ball after the other, and all the time he's talking about vectors and angles and rotation and the pile of money is growing: ten cents, twenty cents, forty cents, and on and on.

Sharkey watched as the pile of coins started to mount up. The poker players started placing side bets on whether or not the Perfesser would miss his shot and forfeit what was starting to be a good pile of change. No one wanted to stop the run.

I got squeezed out as word got out on the street and more of the tough guys started up the stairs. And that's when I thought, these guys are not going to let the Perfesser out of that pool-room with his money. He might not even get out of there with his life! And if some of those characters waited outside, it would be all up with the Perfesser.

What to do? Call the cops? Don't make me laugh! On the Bowery, it wasn't the cops ran things, it was the ones who ran the cops and that was Tammany Hall. No Civil Service in those days, it was the Tammany ward heelers who were the ones to go to for jobs or help in fighting an eviction notice or getting a kid out of jail before the real crooks got to him.

I tried to remember who was the Tammany man around here and came up with the name Sheehan. He wasn't a saloon keeper, like most of them; he was a barber and I found him in his own shop, asleep in his barber chair. He might not have been a saloon keeper himself, but he sure patronized them!

I joggled him awake. "Mr. Sheehan, there's trouble at Sharkey's!"

"There's always trouble at Sharkey's," he muttered. "What's it about?"

"There's a greenhorn, just off the boat, and he's taking down Sharkey for a bundle at pool," I explained. "But this greenhorn's connected to Mr. Edison, who is working for Mr. Morgan," I said. "And if he doesn't get where he's supposed to go, Mr. Morgan might get upset."

I didn't know Morgan from Adam's off ox but I did know that Mr. J.P. Morgan was the one person no one wanted to get upset, not even a Tammany ward heeler. So Sheehan got out of his chair and headed to the precinct while I ran back to Sharkey's to see if I could get the Perfesser out of there before all Hell broke loose and he found himself in jail, instead of at Edison's workshop.

By the time I got back to Sharkey's, the room was packed full. I couldn't see much over the big bodies of men in flashy suits but I could hear the Perfesser announce, "I have completed my task. I thank you for your indulgence." I wiggled through the crowd so I could get to the Perfesser before anyone else did.

He picked up his winnings, which by now had come to quite a pile of coins and greenbacks, made a little bow and headed for the door.

Two of Sharkey's biggest bruisers stopped him. They outweighed him by about a hundred pounds each and it wasn't all fat, either.

"Where do you think you're going?" Sharkey said, nastily, from his throne.

"I am going to the laboratory of Mr. Thomas Edison," said the Perfesser in his persnickety way. "I have an appointment with Mr. Edison concerning his invention of electric generators. I have an improvement that will enable electricity to be brought to the general public."

"Ain't you going to give us a chance to get that money back?"

"I do not think you can," said the Perfesser.

The two bruisers step forward. The Perfesser steps back against the pool table.

I've never been known for fighting, except in the interests of the public welfare, but I did what I had to do. I used my paperbag to whack the nearest bruiser right behind the knees. He tipped over onto the second bruiser. He whacked the first guy, who swung wildly and hit another guy who was just watching the show. He hit back. Next thing you know, everyone was fighting except the Perfesser and me. I grabbed his hand and got him out onto the stairs just as the cops arrived with Sheehan panting behind them. One of the cops yelled "Raid!" and charged in.

The Perfesser and I stepped back and let the cops run up the stairs. Whatever was going on at Sharkey's, I wanted the Perfesser out of it.

Back out on the street, the Perfesser handed me a penny. "I always repay my debts," he said.

"Now you can take the horse-car to where Mr. Edison is working," I told him, pointing to one down the street. "And don't show that wad around. I didn't pull you out of there to get you held up by someone else."

He smiled and patted me on the shoulder. "Young man," he said, "do you ever read the newspapers you sell?"

"Sometimes," I said. It wouldn't do for me to admit that I was a reader.

"You should. You should read everything you can. Reading is very important." He looked around at the people on the street. Those days the Bowery wasn't as bad as it is now, but it wasn't Fifth Avenue, either. There were ladies of loose morals sashaying up and down and their protectors and pickpockets and other low-lifes lounging around along with the rest of the marks and suckers that the pickpockets and low-lifes preyed on. The Perfesser gave me the once-over and said, "You did not have to help me. It was no concern of yours whether I was beaten and robbed." "Maybe." I didn't want to be called a sucker just because I felt sorry for a greenhorn.

"But you did."

"It was the right thing to do."

"You are better than these people." He waved at the low-lifes. "They would have left me to be slaughtered."

"I couldn't do that," I says. "It wouldn't be right."

"Precisely so," said the Perfesser. "You will do what is right. You continue to do what is right and I see you will go far. What is your name, young man?"

"Alfred, but they call me Al. Al Smith." I held out my hand, like a grown man.

"And I am Nikola Tesla," he said, shaking my hand and giving me that little bow of his.

And off he went and he wound up in Edison's workshop like he planned. And the rest of the story you all know, so I won't bore you with it.

✗   ✗   ✗   ✗

So you see, fellas, if it wasn't for me, Dr. Tesla wouldn't never have made it to Edison's lab that first day in New York. Of course, he couldn't let people know that he got the money hustling pool. That wouldn't look right, not for an educated man like Dr. Tesla, so he came up with the machine story.

I met him again, a lot later, first when I was in the legislature and then when I was governor. I never let on that I was the newsie who got him into and out of Sharkey's on his first day in New York. But I remembered what he said about reading and that he thought I could do better than be a bum on the Bowery, and I made sure that his idea about bringing electricity to everyone happened.

And if anyone prints this story about how Tesla hustled pool on the Bowery and Al Smith got him out of a fight, I'll deny every bit of it.

Roberta Rogow is a retired Children's Librarian living in New Jersey, who writes historical mysteries, although she sometimes twists the history. Her most recent book, *Mischief in Manatas*, continues the adventures of Halvar the Hireling, an ex-mercenary in a re-imagined colonial Manhattan, run by Spanish moors instead of Dutch traders.

A BUSINESS PROPOSITION

by Janice Law

"There's always money." Irene picked a thread from her blond cashmere sweater. "You've always said, 'there's always money somewhere.'"

"Honey," Stu said, "there's always money: we just don't have enough of it."

Irene's face took on a truculent expression. They'd had this same conversation before they put the house on the market, and though Stu had prepared himself for the inevitable fireworks, he felt his stomach clench.

"Adult orthodontia," Irene said. "That's the growth market."

"That *was* the growth market. Sweetheart, everyone's retrenching. As you know from your shop." Irene ran Phlox Frocks, which had done well for eight years then started to fade.

"Don't call me 'sweetheart' when you're trying to take the roof from our heads."

"Don't be melodramatic. I'm just talking about a little retrenching of our own."

"You're talking bankruptcy," Irene said coldly.

Stu felt the headache which had been lurking just behind his ears dig in its claws. "It's been eight months," he said. "Not a nibble. We've reduced the price twice."

"It's a super property," Irene said stubbornly.

"Gorgeous. I love it. We just can't afford it. It's a strictly business proposition."

From his seat on the oversized leather sofa, Stu looked out the French doors to the pool and cabana. Inside, anchoring the thirty-foot living room, was a massive custom-built fireplace. They had to spritz the lichens growing on the stones to keep their leathery foliage alive. "A really special touch," their decorator assured him.

Upstairs were five bedrooms and six baths, one with Jacuzzi. The kitchen had a professional range and fridge, wall oven, and designer lighting; the exterior featured a slate roof and fieldstone facing on the front façade. All super. All expensive. All making for a major depression.

Now that they were in financial difficulty, Stu sometimes wondered at their acquisitions: the carved carousel horses, Shaker bureaus, Colonial silver, French country beds. A shared delight in treasure hunting and bargains had been the glue of their marriage, and new possessions kept Irene happy. Stu was beginning to wonder how well she'd manage on thrift and dispersal.

He realized she was saying something about a new line for the shop, about new suppliers in Guatemala and Mexico where wages were rock bottom.

"The house," Stu interrupted, "is mortgaged to the hilt. And then there's my office building. The balloon payment is coming due in six months."

"We might sell the office building," Irene said, although she must have known that was ridiculous.

"And turn around and pay rent for my practice and give up the tenants' rents? We can only survive financially if we aren't carrying this house. We need a smaller place, maybe a condo, for a few years."

"But we can't sell this house," Irene said implacably. "As you know."

"We may have to reduce the price," Stu said. "Come down a little farther. Give Lonnie more wiggle room with buyers."

"We're not going to take a loss." It was one of the principles of Irene's universe that property always increases in value.

"We need to get rid of the house," Stu repeated.

Right then there was a pause, a long pause, which was how they hesitated at the edge of the abyss that divided ordinary life from—well, not quite so ordinary life.

"It's all insured," Irene said, and Stu felt a little ripple of fear and excitement.

"Policy up to date?" he asked. But he knew the answer. Insurance was another of Irene's polestars.

She nodded her head without speaking, and just like that, although he didn't quite understand how they'd gotten to where they were, Stu knew they'd decided and only the details were left. Complicated details, as it turned out.

"They can test, you know," Irene said. "For accelerants and gasoline and things. They even have dogs. We'll have to be careful."

Stu was a little surprised that Irene knew so much about arson. He could smell the wood ashes in the fireplace; when it was cool at night, they often had a fire. "It can't be that hard to have a building fire."

"It is in houses like this one," said Irene.

Stu realized glumly that she was right. Their dream house came equipped with smoke, carbon monoxide, and radon detectors and a whole array of sophisticated security.

Then there was the furniture. The last of the big Shaker pieces would have to be saved, Irene insisted. It was museum quality—and her collection of majolica! She couldn't bear to lose that.

Her mouth trembled as she spoke, and Stu felt a film of sweat forming beneath his fine knit shirt. "We could go to jail for arson," he said. In the back of his mind, he was counting on fear to save them.

Irene set her face, showing a strong jaw and a thin, determined mouth. "We have the house on the market. We're moving to a smaller place. We're putting some things in storage, that's all."

"The majolica and the Shaker bureau," he said, realizing that he would have to compromise. "Insurance can take care of the rest."

"We might check our coverage," Irene said. "Some things have appreciated over the last few years."

"Changes to the policy would look suspicious—if we do it," he added, because he, Stu, would have to make the hard decisions and keep a cool head.

"We will do it," Irene said. "And, anyway, there are *specialists*. We wouldn't need to be involved." Specialist was one of her favorite words. That he was a specialist in orthodonture had been one of Stu's attractions.

"Specialists are expensive," he observed, his heart stuttering.

"You've always said 'you have to spend money to make money,'" Irene said, and when Stu reluctantly assented, Irene mentioned Vinnie, their haulage contractor. "Vinnie will know someone in 'insurance.'"

A week later, after Irene spent a quarter of an hour bemoaning the property market downturn to Vinnie, a plain dark blue van pulled up on the Klopper's fine gravel driveway. Hector—"No last name, please"—got out. He was a cheerful, round-faced man with an ebullient manner, who bounced on the balls of his feet like a boxer. Hector poked his nose into the closets, inspected the basement and the attic, checked the garage, and appraised the security systems with a professional eye.

"Fine place you've got here," he said. His black eyes twinkled. "Top flight security."

"Thirty-thousand dollars worth," Stu said.

"Really?" Hector looked around again as if surprised, so that Stu had a moment's anxiety that they'd been overcharged.

"A robbery wouldn't do?" Hector inquired, stroking his short, thick mustache. "I mean a really top flight, professional job. Lighten you of all these antiques, *objects d'art*, assorted pretty things?"

Stu shook his head. "The property market's in the can. We need to get major cash out of this place."

"Oh, *comprendez*," said Hector. "An absolute bitch of a property market. But I want you to be sure. I want you to be satisfied. People get attached to houses and furniture," he added. His deep voice turned melancholy and his mobile face took on an almost clerical cast at the vanity of earthly things. "Foolish, of course." He smiled at Stu, man to man. "You'll know better. In my experience, men know better than to set their hearts on real estate. The Missus, now, is different. The Missus in these jobs is always the problem. So I ask you to be sure, okay?"

Stu cleared his throat. "We're going to put a few of the more valuable things in storage. We've got the house on the market, after all."

"Good thought! You can't put a price on sentiment, can you? But not too much, Stu. That's a dead giveaway. I can leave you a clean site—absolutely no incriminating traces—but you gotta cooperate. You strip the house, that's bad business. Particularly should you put in for insurance on stuff that's in storage. That's greed, see, and I wind up taking the risks for it. You understand what I'm saying, Stu?"

Stu thought he would rather be called 'Dr. Klopper' and disliked Hector's air of conspiratorial intimacy, but he was wary of taking offense. Instead, he cleared his throat and said, "A couple of Shaker pieces and our majolica collection. That's all."

"Good choices!" Hector was enthusiastic. "Especially the big bureau. Very nice. Very nice, indeed. And majolica: always cheerful! But remember, Stu, something has to be sacrificed in this. This is not free money. Excuse me for reminding an intelligent man such as yourself, but this is a precision business."

Stu nodded his head. Hector was beginning to exhaust him.

"So, okay! We're on." There was a subtle shift in Hector's tone. "I'll need $5,000 in cash up front. Small bills. I recommend right out of your business receipts, Stu. You don't want a large withdrawal showing on your bank account."

"No, indeed." Stu hadn't even thought about his bank statement. He was a specialist of a different sort altogether, and he suspected that this business was beyond him. He should have left Hector to Irene, who seemed energized by the whole thing.

"You and the Missus go off on vacation," Hector continued, "a couple days away—say, within the next two weeks? You set it up and call me from a public phone when you're ready. And *puleeze!* No cellular, no home, no office phone. Give me dates and times. Here's where you can call. Just ask for Hector. I'll take care of everything. But, Stu, the main thing: as soon as the job's done, I expect the other $5,000. Pronto."

"Sure," Stu said, though even the first installment would be a struggle. But afterwards there would be plenty. Afterwards, they'd be out of the woods, able to regroup, home free. Even if he had to float a short-term loan, max out some new credit cards.

"I stress the time frame," Hector continued, "so that there's no misunderstanding. Sometimes in these particular cases, people are in more of a rush to get things done than they are to pay for them. This is unbusinesslike, as I don't need to tell you, Stu. I always say, I'm in no hurry to do the job. You need more time to get your cash together, you let me know; we delay the whole project. A week, a month, more—it doesn't matter to me. But when it's done, it's done and paid for. You understand this, Stu?"

"Of course," he said.

"Good, great! Now let me go over everything again with you, because we don't want any mistakes." Hector sat down on one of the pale suede sofas and spelled everything out for Stu, who felt his headache come rampaging back. When they'd decided to go ahead and to hire a specialist, Stu had enjoyed a brief fantasy of liberation, but there was something so real and solid about Hector that Stu felt profoundly depressed.

"I don't know about this," he said to Irene later.

"What don't you know?" She was loading her favorite china into the station wagon. She already had a Jasper Johns print and a little Milton Avery canvas hidden under a good antique quilt.

"This Hector guy."

"We can manage him," Irene said.

"We don't understand about any of this stuff. We don't know if he's any good or whether we can trust him."

"He doesn't know if he can trust us, either," Irene said calmly. She had taken to criminality with an ease that Stu would never have anticipated.

"I'm going to bring the van home tomorrow," she said. "For some of the small furniture."

"We can't be sentimental about these things," Stu said. "They're all insured and it's got to look like an accident."

"That's Hector's job," Irene said. "We're paying him—God! We're *overpaying* him—to make it look right. Our job is to maximize the profits. Just so we *can* pay him."

"I've gotten another credit card," Stu said. "We'll get a cash advance."

"That will look nice on the record."

"For our little getaway holiday."

"What about the second installment? A ten-thousand dollar getaway stretches credibility."

Stu's head hammered again, but he told himself that Hector was a businessman, after all. No one in business today expects cash on demand. Payment on delivery was just a manner of speaking. "He'll just have to wait for the settlement," Stu said. "There'll be some emergency money. There'll have to be."

⚡ ⚡ ⚡ ⚡

The Kloppers left on a Thursday evening, drove as far as Barnstable and reached Provincetown for lunch the next day. The summer crowds had departed, leaving early dusk and sea mist and a chilly wind that blew over the dunes and slopped the harbor water against the pilings. Stu and Irene ate an expensive dinner in a drafty restaurant. They both drank too much; she seemed exhilarated; he felt depressed. Neither one could resist checking the front desk to see if there were any messages.

Friday night passed and Saturday and Saturday night.

"He's a fraud. He's not really going to do it." Irene was angry, but Stu felt relieved.

"Maybe that would be just as well," he said, for he had begun to have regrets for the beautiful house they'd planned so carefully.

"We'd be back where we were minus $5,000," Irene reminded him tartly. "You were the one who brought up the idea in the first place."

After arguing about that until Stu's stomach turned sour, they went to bed. The phone woke them like a siren at 3 a.m. It was the Dover Crossing fire chief to say there'd been a devastating blaze. Stu confirmed that no one was in the house and said they'd return immediately. He was surprised at how shocked he felt, how cold and shaky.

He and Irene stopped on the road to notify the insurance company and managed Dover Crossing by early afternoon. The whole neighborhood stank of smoke, and water stood in the gutters from the fire hoses. Their lawn was ruined, that's what struck Stu first, the professionally-pampered grass rutted and churned to mud by the fire trucks. Shrubbery was singed and broken, one tree was burned—and then nothing but a great heap of burned wood and slates with only the custom fireplace—"solid as a rock," the artisan had joked—blackened, its lichens dead, thrusting indomitably from the rubble of two and a half floors and the roof timbers.

"God," said Irene. "It looks like a bomb site."

Spurred by the potential magnitude of the claim, the insurance agent arrived Monday morning. Davison Murdock was a dark, silky-voiced man with beautiful long fingers and a strong scent of cologne. He clucked quietly to himself as he inspected the ruin and wrote voluminous notes in a big red vinyl binder. He assured the Kloppers that a full investigation would be made. Of course, they'd want to know what happened. "Such a beautiful house. A real tragedy," he said.

On four hours of sleep, Stu couldn't tell if the agent was being obtuse or ironic. "We've been wiped out."

"I'm working to process your claim as quickly as possible," Murdock said with just the faintest hint of reproach. He shook his head at the charred timbers, the water-filled pits, the cracked and blackened slates. "A real shame." He pushed a board with one foot and made another note.

Next, Mr. Murdock inquired about the furniture. Irene wiped away her tears and produced the snaps she'd retrieved first thing from their safe deposit box.

"Everything was in the house?"

"Except the big Shaker bureau. We had it in storage. We were thinking of selling it—museum quality pieces have appreciated so much in value."

Stu noticed that she didn't mention the majolica or any of the other valuables.

Out back, the roof of the cabana was singed and the water in the perfect sapphire pool was speckled with soot and soft bits of drowned wood.

"This can all be cleaned up," the insurance agent said briskly. "But the house—well, you know that's a total loss, and with the way construction costs have gone up, you'll probably have to modify your design."

"We were in the process of moving," Stu said. "The house was on the market."

"Really?" The insurance agent's smooth, brown face tightened ever so slightly, and Irene had the sense to burst into tears.

"How could we stay here now, anyway? I couldn't bear it!" Her tears were all the more convincing since she'd forgotten to pack up the very nice Japanese prints in the guest room.

"We'll want to start again fresh. Somewhere else in town. Or out of town. I don't feel the same about Dover Crossing anymore." Stu put his arm around Irene protectively, adding, "I don't think my wife is up to this today." He certainly didn't feel up to it, either. Not today, not ever.

"Losing your home is a terrible thing," the agent said. "Terrible. We'll do everything we can to expedite your claim and make it easier." He shook hands, made sure they had his card, and said he'd call them at the motel just as soon as the paperwork was finished.

"We'd have been better to have taken the house off the market," Irene said when they got into their car. "You see how he picked up on that? I don't trust him."

"We always knew there'd be an investigation," Stu said. "We always knew that. Just as long as it's a short one."

Monday afternoon, Stu had a call from Hector, who spoke of punctuality. Stu spoke of arrangements and emergency cash and the costs of the local Ramada Inn and restaurant meals. Tuesday and Wednesday, Stu canceled all his appointments, badgered the insurance people, and snooped around after the arson squad. Thursday, Hector called the motel. Stu started to explain and delay.

"Sell the majolica," Hector interrupted. "Half the collection, maybe. I can put you in touch with someone who can move it fast for you. You need to move fast on this matter, Stu."

"Listen, the settlement will be along any day now. There's no need for us to take a loss just for a few days."

Hector pointed out that he was the only one taking a loss and hung up. Stu's head began to throb quietly.

✗   ✗   ✗   ✗

On Friday, Irene took a thousand out of the till at Phlox Frocks, called Hector and made the first installment. When she returned, she wore a serious expression.

"Wasn't he pleased?" Stu asked. "He must know we're doing our best."

"He thinks because we paid him some, we can pay him the rest."

"We will, we will," Stu said.

"He knows where we've stored the furniture, too," Irene said. "We're going to have to move it."

"What's he going to do? Steal it?"

"He mentioned the insurance company. 'You're dealing with Davison Murdock, aren't you?' he says to me. 'I know Murdock. All he'd need would be just one word: Acme Self Storage. That would do. You wouldn't have to tell old Murdock another thing.'"

"Jesus!" said Stu and his heart gave a panicky leap. "We could sell one of the paintings. But how soon we'd get the money..."

"They're already in on the claim," Irene said.

"The majolica, then," Stu said. "We've got to do it." He held out for that, although Irene was furious and tried tears. In the end, he took another day off work and drove to a New York antiques dealer who specialized in majolica. He returned with sixty-five hundred dollars and a nagging headache.

"The plates were worth more," she said.

"We'll get the settlement," Stu said. "I'm thinking we go south, somewhere like Hilton Head or Naples. You could open a nice shop."

Images of nice shops, clean beaches, happy couples, tennis courts, golf greens—and wealthy kids with crooked teeth—flitted through Stu's imagination. In such a paradise, good things would be possible, and when the check finally came, he felt the future open.

There was only the lot to be sold. Irene arranged for a contractor to truck away the debris and fill in the old foundation, and she got a lawn company to level and seed the lawn. "A beautiful lot," she said. "Mature trees. Someone's just got to buy it."

She thought they could sell the lot themselves—that was Irene's idea of thrift—and they spent their weekends showing prospective buyers around the property. One damp November day, when they'd just said good-bye to a couple up from New York City, a little dark blue van pulled into the driveway. Hector joined them on the tiled pool deck beside the cabana.

"Well, nice job," said Hector. "Looks like a park. Me, I can visualize a house right about here. Terrace, big porch. Classic, you know. Old money looks for new money wallets. Am I right?"

"Perhaps you're buying," Irene said. "Or not in your income bracket?"

"Now that's unkind," he said. "And unkind is unwise, I always think. You and the Mr. got away with this scam—despite some foolish moves."

"I don't know why you're here," Stu said. When his forehead started hammering and his gut tightened up in the bad old way, he realized that he'd almost gotten used to living relaxed and tension-free.

"Interest, Stu," Hector said. "You will remember I was quite explicit on two matters: prompt payment and an honest job. Now I find there was neither. This does not make me happy."

"You'd have looted the stuff and sold it," Irene said sharply.

Hector was imperturbable. "Sure, these jobs have certain perks. But remember, I take all the risk in them. Now, I'm a craftsman. Murdock and your local arson squad investigators found squat. But they're suspicious and their suspicions are focused my way. I've got to keep a low profile around here for a while. That means a monetary loss. See what I'm saying? Certain perks of the job are essential, that's all."

"He wants money," said Irene. Stu didn't say anything. He could feel a darkness settling over his field of vision and an odd, roaring sound in his ears.

"Shall we say interest due and a little bonus? Maybe another five."

"You wish," said Irene.

"Lyme Specialty Movers and Storage," Hector said. "Where three crates formerly in Acme Self Storage now repose. How's that? Information your insurance agent and the arson squad would like? Or not?"

"You're not getting the money," said Stu loudly.

"Now, Stu, this is a business proposition and this is a business mistake you're making."

Stu hit him then, or rather, from Stu's perspective, his fist suddenly shot out and caught Hector on the side of the head. Hector backed away, but Stu swung again and though he slipped to his knees on the damp tiles, he connected solidly. Hector gave a little cry as his head hit the raised lip of the pool, and Stu crawled over and pushed him into the empty blue basin.

There was a thump; pain shot through Stu's bruised knees, and he thought to himself *That will do it! That will send him packing*. He gasped for breath, aware of the traffic and crows and the faint, rainy patter of the wind, but he didn't hear Hector. There was silence from that region, broken when Irene said, "Oh, God, I don't think he's moving."

"Nonsense," said Stu. "It's maybe eight feet." He leaned over the edge of the pool and saw that there was something nasty about the way Hector was lying.

"You'd better go down," said Irene.

A little water reflected the November sky through an archipelago of fallen leaves. Stu descended reluctantly, envisioning another undignified scuffle. Still, Hector's posture was odd, and when Stu knelt on the cement, his hand went out of itself and touched the carotid artery and felt warm, silent, motionless flesh.

Stu sat back on his heels in the deep end of his empty swimming pool, unable to imagine how this had happened. Instead, his mind focused on the pool, which like so many other things that had once been important now seemed useless.

Irene climbed down beside him, awkward in her high heels.

"He's not dead," she said.

Stu nodded, unable to speak.

Irene denied this; she had a deep sense of entitlement, as if fate were obliged to smooth her way. That seemed rather funny in the circumstances, and Stu started to laugh.

"Stop that," Irene said. "We don't have time." She grabbed Hector's arms and dragged him toward the shallow end.

"Not through the water," Stu cried, for he still had some dim idea of outrage, of evidence, of calling the proper authorities.

"We can't carry him up the ladder."

By the time they got Hector up onto the pool deck, Stu had lost all initiative. When Irene said, "The foundation," he dragged the body over to the soft, dented earth.

"This was my office," he remarked to no one in particular, while Irene began a frantic search for a spade.

Eventually she found an old snow shovel stuck in the back of the cabana, and Stu began the excavation.

The ground was wet from the fall rains, and that and the thin aluminum snow shovel made digging slow, heavy, muddy work even in new fill. Stu's pants were smeared with earth from the knees down and his good loafers were full of mud before Irene agreed the hole was deep enough. They wrestled Hector to the edge and shoved him in, but their excavation wasn't quite long enough at the bottom, so that Hector landed awkwardly, with one knee bent and one foot in the air and one open eye fixed glassily upon them.

"We can't leave him like that," Stu cried. It seemed impossible to believe that he had done this terrible thing.

"Do you think we have all day?" Irene snatched the shovel away, kicked off her heels and started heaving earth into the hole. She'd covered the body with a few inches of dirt, when they realized that they didn't have the van keys. Stu had to jump into the hole and dig through the wet earth to reach Hector's pockets. He climbed out, dripping wet with nerves and shivering uncontrollably.

Irene worked until the snow shovel snapped; then they used their hands and feet. Kicking and shoving at the sandy earth, Stu realized that the details of a thing are what kill you. Almost anything is imaginable until you come to the details.

When they were finished with the grave and had gotten themselves cleaned up, the Kloppers abandoned Hector's van in Bridgeport.

"He's gone," Irene said when they returned to Dover Crossing. "We don't have to worry."

"He's gone," Stu repeated.

"For as long as we hold the lot," Irene said.

Stu scowled. "I don't think we can afford just to hold the lot."

"Build on it, then," said Irene.

Stu gave a nervous giggle. "Take Hector's idea and put a terrace over the old office space."

"It faces north," Irene said taking up the idea without even a shiver, "but very nice in the summer."

Stu could feel his head starting to throb. Southern paradises faded like old tourist brochures. They'd never leave Dover Crossing now; they'd never be rid of the house.

Irene, however, was warming to the idea. "A smaller house, have them open up only part of the old foundation. We'd be sure, then."

And though Stu resisted, that's what they did. Come spring, they put up a pseudo-French style with brick walls and a slate roof, a really nice house, which they felt they deserved, but which was a little more than they could afford.

Shortly after they moved in, Stu arrived home one day to see a *Vinceni's Refuse Removal* truck parked in the driveway. He remembered right away that Vinnie, the haulage contractor, was Hector's cousin.

Stu dawdled getting into the house. He put the car in the garage, checked the security system, poured himself a beer. Meanwhile, Irene was talking all the time to Vinnie in the living room. Finally, Stu heard her say, "Come back tomorrow night and we'll straighten everything out."

"You understand," Vinnie said, "a business proposition."

"Sure thing," Irene said. Stu thought she sounded almost cheerful. When Vinnie was gone, Stu found Irene looking thoughtful.

"Trouble?" Stu asked. He could see it all now. Not only were they trapped forever in Dover Crossing, but they'd never be out of the financial woods. Never.

Irene smiled at him. "It's a good thing we didn't finish the little terrace," she said. In her untroubled, even faintly excited expression, Stu recognized that his wife had become a stranger to him and that his marriage had acquired a new and terrible basis.

Stu could not immediately resign himself to this order of things. He was still Dr. Klopper, a *specialist*, a reliable and honorable man, an ordinary guy, who'd just had some reverses and bad luck. "No! Don't even think it!"

Irene's eyes narrowed. "Really, Stu," she said. "This is business. This is strictly a business proposition."

⚔

Janice Law writes novels and non-fiction as well as short stories. Her most recent book is the Lambda mystery finalist, *Moon over Tangier* featuring the gay, alcoholic painter, Francis Bacon. It is the last volume of a trilogy published by Mysteriouspress.com. She lives with her husband, a sportswriter, in Connecticut.

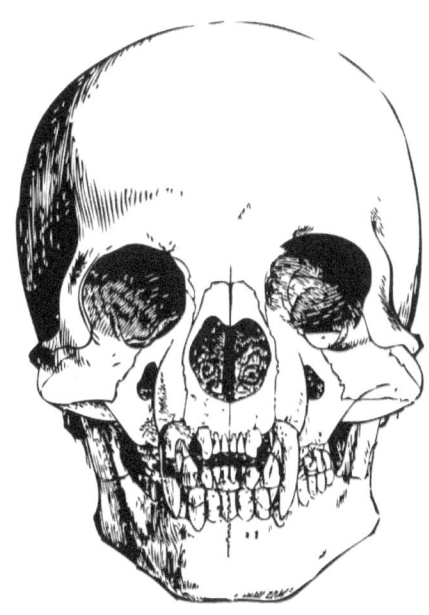

A KING'S RANSOM

by John M. Floyd

Sheriff Lucy Valentine looked up from her desk telephone as her mother Fran stomped through the open doorway of the office. This was not always a cause for celebration: the sheriff loved her mom, but they seldom agreed on much of anything. Fran's favorite topics of discussion were Lucy's love for Hostess Twinkies, her dislike for exercise, and her apparent disinterest in the whole idea of marriage and grandchildren. For once, though, Lucy was relieved to see her.

"Your message said you needed me," Fran said, looking suspicious.

"I did," Lucy admitted. "I still do. Remember a girl named Tina King?"

"Sure. She was captain of the junior academic team when I helped coach them." Fran dropped into a chair. "She's what, a senior now?"

"Freshman in college, according to her dad."

"Her dad?" Fran said. "What's happened?"

Lucy leaned back in her desk chair and rubbed her eyes. She wondered if she looked as tired as she felt.

"Tina was abducted this afternoon."

"What?!"

"While jogging in the neighborhood, apparently." Lucy pointed to her notes. "She was home from school for the weekend. The kidnapper phoned her family about an hour ago—her father got it on tape."

"What do you mean on tape?"

"He's a lawyer, says he records all his calls. He just e-mailed me the audio. Listen to this."

Lucy picked up her iPhone, punched a key, and cranked up the volume. A male's gravelly voice filled the room. Fran grabbed a pencil and pad from Lucy's desktop.

The caller said that he'd taken Tina captive, then he listed ransom demands—half a million dollars to be delivered tonight to an unobservable spot just east of town—and said the two of them were parked someplace where they couldn't be found. He added that he would allow Tina to send one message to her family as proof that she was unharmed. After a short pause, a girl's trembling voice said:

"This is my message: 'Bye, Ned—I can just see you in Italy. And tell your old Army G.P.—Red Grant—to share a key.'"

The call was then disconnected.

Fran finished writing and looked up from her notepad. "That's it?"

"That's it," the sheriff said. "I have no idea what it means—I've played it ten times. Her dad says it makes no sense to him either. By the way, I've also notified the state police and they're on their way."

"Can you locate his phone? What's it called—triangulation?"

"The state cops said they'd try. But I bet he's switched it off."

"Where are Tina's parents at the moment?"

"Sitting by their telephone, waiting," Lucy said. "Any thoughts?"

"About the call?" Fran used the eraser end of the pencil to scratch her head. "Well…. First of all, the kidnapper's not very smart—he revealed that they're 'parked' someplace in a car, which was a mistake, and he let Tina say too much, which was a bigger mistake. Second, Tina King is *super* smart, maybe the most intelligent kid I ever knew. We often used puzzles—hard puzzles—as exercises before competitions and Tina loved that. She always solved them, lightning fast."

"So?"

"So I don't think it's *supposed* to make sense."

Lucy frowned. "What she said, you mean?"

"Yeah. I think Tina's telling us something in her message. She's feeding us clues."

"What kind of clues?"

"Think about it. If you're abducted and your kidnapper gives you a chance to say something quick to your family, do you wish someone else *bon voyage* and chat about the Army, and keys?" Fran shook her head. "No. Tina knows me, knew that her dad would record this, knew that he would call you and probably figured that you'd call me and play this for me. Remember when Penny Collins was snatched a couple years ago? Remember she gave us enough clues to find her? Same kind of thing here: Tina's trying to tell us where she is."

Lucy frowned, thinking that over. "If that's true… then where is she?"

"Don't know yet," Fran said. "But I do know most of her family and friends and I don't know any Ned, or a 'G.P.'—whatever that is—named Red Grant."

"Red Grant was a villain in a James Bond novel. *From Russia With Love*, I think."

Fran ignored her, silently studying the notes she'd jotted down during the playback of the call.

"The movie version, too," Lucy added. "If it matters."

More silence.

Guess not, Lucy thought.

"'Bye, Ned?'" Fran murmured. "What does that part mean? Could it be something else? Buy Ned, maybe? Pie Ned? Pine Ed?"

Suddenly her eyes widened.

"Pine head," she said softly. "Italy…"

Fran turned and looked through the open door of the office. "Charlotte!" she called to the sheriff's assistant. "Phone the movie theatre. Find out what's playing there."

"You mean the one at the mall?" Lucy interrupted.

"Do you know of another one?" Fran said. Outside in the reception area, Charlotte was already dialing.

A moment later Charlotte Hudson put her palm over the phone receiver, scooted her chair back from her desk, and called to Fran, "Four features, some new, some old: *The Maze Runner*, *Interstellar*, *High Noon*, and *Pinocchio*."

Fran nodded, apparently satisfied. "I thought I saw in the paper that it was playing there. Besides, the mall's only a couple miles from the drop-off point."

"What was playing there?" Lucy asked, thoroughly confused. "*From Russia With Love*?"

"*Pinocchio*." Fran turned to her daughter. "Get your deputies over to the mall, Lucy. Tell them you'll give 'em more info shortly."

"What kind of info?"

"I told you, Tina likes puzzles." Fran tapped her temple with a forefinger. "The phrase 'pine head,' in Italian, is 'Pinocchio.' And 'I can see you now?' Since we know they're in a parked car, I bet Tina's telling us that she's somewhere in that mall parking lot, in sight of that theatre marquee."

"But… it's Saturday, Mother. Even if you're right, there could be dozens of cars there. How—"

"We'll have to narrow it down. The words Army, G.P., Grant, the rest—I think it's all in there in the things she told us if we can figure it out."

"All of *what* is in there?"

"What we need to find her," Fran said. "Go ahead and get your men positioned."

Lucy radioed the deputies and got them moving. She told them to park just out of sight of the theatre lot and stand by for more instructions.

For the next several minutes both mother and daughter kept silent. Fran's face had taken on the steady frown that Lucy knew meant she was thinking hard. The sheriff clenched her sweaty hands, waiting and watching.

Then Fran's face cleared, and she smiled. "I think I've got it."

"Got what?"

"Remember the message? 'Red Grant? Share a key?'"

"What about it?"

In a calm but urgent voice, Fran told Lucy her theory. Lucy listened carefully, then snatched up the radio and passed along the new information to her deputies.

When Lucy signed off, Fran said, "Should we go, too?"

"No—they're already close. Now that they know what to look for, they'll either see it or not and contact us. I'll call Tina's dad and let him know what's happening, then let's wait here."

Sure enough, three minutes later the radio crackled. Deputy Ed Malone reported that they had indeed spotted the kidnapper parked with a teenaged girl in a red 1998 Jeep on one end of the lot outside the mall theatre. Malone recognized Tina, had seen that the man in the car looked distracted and decided to move in fast. It was risky, but it worked. The suspect was taken completely by surprise—he wasn't even armed—and was now in custody. Tina was okay.

This time Fran and the sheriff didn't wait. They jumped into a patrol car and roared to the scene. Five minutes later, they were standing there in the parking lot with a safe but shaken Tina King. The suspect sat cuffed and sullen in the back seat of Malone's cruiser while Sheriff Valentine phoned Tina's parents again with the good news. The freed kidnappee wiped a tear from her eye and hugged both Lucy and Fran.

"Good work, young lady," the sheriff told her.

Tina gave her a weak smile. "You, too."

"Me?" Lucy shook her head. "My mother here's the one who figured it out."

Tina's smile widened. "But you're the one who called her in. I'm glad you did."

"I am, too." Lucy folded her arms, looking back and forth between Fran and Tina. "Okay—which one of you's gonna tell me *how* it got figured out?"

Tina King gave Fran a sly look. Fran grinned and said to Lucy, "Tina's message didn't just tell us where her abductor's car was parked—it told us what it looked like." As if to emphasize this, she pointed to the car in question.

"You said that already. But *how*?"

"The word 'Jeep' comes from the Army's abbreviation—G.P.— for 'general purpose' vehicle," Fran said. "If you then combine 'old,' 'Red,' 'Grant,' and 'share a key,' you get—"

"An older-model Jeep Grand Cherokee," Lucy said as the pieces fell into place. She found herself staring at the suspect's car. "Red in color."

Both Fran and Tina nodded.

Lucy took a moment to absorb this. Do brilliant people's brains really work this way? she wondered.

Tina grinned as if reading her mind. "You've gotta love puzzles," she said with a shrug.

Lucy faced her again. "Let me get this straight. The guy told you he would let you call your dad...."

"Right. So he'd know it was me."

"And how much time did you have before the call to plan what you would say? To make up the 'clues?'"

"A couple minutes." Tina said. "It was enough."

"But—as odd as your message was—weren't you afraid your kidnapper'd be suspicious?"

"Not really." All of them shot a glance at the handcuffed suspect. He just sat there in the patrol car looking more bored than worried. "He wasn't mean to me or anything," Tina added—"but he's not too bright."

The sheriff shook her head in wonder. "Looks like Mother was correct. *You're* the one who's bright."

Tina smiled again, this time at Fran. "So is she."

John M. Floyd's stories have recently appeared in *AHMM*, *EQMM*, *The Strand*, *Woman's World*, *TheSaturday Evening Post*, and *The Best American Mystery Stories 2015*. A former Air Force captain and IBM systems engineer, John won a Derringer Award in 2007 and was nominated for an Edgar in 2015.

RUNNING IN PLACE

by J.E. Irvin

I stood by the scale built into the floor of the Hamilton County Morgue waiting for Sean Farley's dead weight to register. The needle settled at one-eighty. Farley, expired less than twenty-four hours, was thirty pounds leaner than his high school playing days, a decorated Afghanistan war hero found dead during the alleged commission of a crime. He couldn't bully his way out of this one. I resisted the surge of old memories. Maybe I'd stroll down the nostalgia trail later. Right now, it was lunchtime.

Rolling the gurney through the door of the cold box, I lifted the sack containing Farley's possessions and deposited it on the shelf below the one holding that half-full bottle of Canadian rye. My mouth watered. With a nod at the bottle, I wheeled Farley's corpse to the back of the room, checked the thermometer to be sure the temperature still held steady at forty degrees and flicked off the lights. "Where there's no hope," I whispered, "there's no hurry."

Down the hall, the answering machine light blinked, lighting my office with a weird red flicker. I retrieved my brown bag from the bottom desk drawer and settled into Doc Harrington's cracked leather chair, the one he passed down to me when he retired. The ham sandwich from the deli down the block tasted of old bread and dry cheese. I really wanted a drink, but I wasn't yet ready to share space with Farley. I'd have plenty of time during the autopsy to address the dead son-of-a bitch. Besides, one of my investigators might show up early and ask to observe. I preferred to conduct this examination by myself.

Swiveling in the chair, I stared out at the parking lot. Bob Watson, the transporter on call, had backed the hearse halfway under the awning that protected the entry door. Tiny ice pellets bounced and rolled off the hood. Wondering when he'd be back, I pressed the retrieve button on the machine and listened to my calls.

"*Al? Courtney here. I'm off to Carlotti's for a sandwich. Got the notes from the Farley crime scene. I'll bring them to you after lunch.*"

Beep.

"*Doctor Harding? Srithan Moonda from the Journal Herald. Any results on the Farley autopsy? Sheriff Houston says they found the body on the floor of Compton's Jewelry Store at two a.m. this morning. Very strange, don't you think? I'll call back later.*"

"Strange?" I mouthed the words around a bite of potato chip. "Not if you knew Farley. And you're crazy, Moonda, if you think I'm telling you anything."

Beep.

"*Alan?*" A deep breath. A sigh. Brianna Campbell. Farley's ex-fiancée. Everybody's old flame. Trouble. "*I really need to talk to you. Sean left me a message I don't understand. Please. Call me when you get this.*"

The intercom buzzer bleated. Startled, I leaned forward and all the folders on my desk flew toward the floor. Reaching for the com link, I pressed it down and barked, "Who is it?"

A voice on the other end, Brianna's voice, asked, "Alan?"

My hand shook. "No," I said, "this is a recording."

"Don't be stupid," Brianna snapped. "Let me in."

"I'm working, Brianna."

She ignored me, just like always. "I know you're on break. I really have to talk to you."

I checked my watch. Halfway through the lunch hour. I pushed the door release button, gathered up the fallen files and headed for the reception area.

She was looking at the photos of crime scenes lining the corridor, her auburn curls tucked beneath a wool cap, the collar of her down jacket pulled up around the large silver hoops, her signature jewelry item. Those water-color blue eyes of hers skewered me as I moved to her side.

"You know I can't discuss Sean's case," I said, running a hand through my thinning crew cut so I wouldn't touch her cheek.

"What did you say to Sean?"

"Me?" I fiddled with the pencil holder on the hall desk. "Not much. We haven't exactly been on the best of terms."

"But you were talking to him," she insisted. She pulled out her cell phone and held it up so I could read the saved message. *H's a genius, P's a rat. I'm the one you'll love when this is over.*

"No new information there, Bri," I told her. "Sean always thought he'd win you back in the end."

"But he knew Pat and I had, well, gotten engaged. Sort of. And he was talking to you. I saw you at the stadium, on the running track."

I glanced at the closed door of the cold box and thought about Pat Houston, county sheriff and an even bigger idiot than Farley. Back in '99, he played center to Farley's quarterback while I caught Hail Mary passes in the end zone and waited for Brianna to come to her senses and pick me. Never happened.

"Don't turn a sighting into a conspiracy, Bri." I looked up to see her picking at her fingernails. Several curlicues of pink polish littered the scuffed linoleum floor. "I run every day. Farley just happened to show up one Saturday. He turned it into a habit for all of two weeks."

She nodded. Sean Farley's short attention span was legend. Then she changed direction. "Pat says there are diamonds missing."

"Pat shouldn't be talking to you about any of this." I looked up, hoping the shuffling noise down the hall meant my investigator, Courtney Pillow, had returned and I could cut this conversation short.

"One of them was the diamond Pat was planning to give me."

I heard a hiccup in her voice, the sound of old loss trying to break through the new disappointment. Farley had given her a ring once, then taken it back when he found out she had cheated with Pat. Brianna so wanted to be claimed by someone. Too bad she never wanted that someone to be me.

"Alan?" Courtney poked her ear-muffed salt-and-pepper head around the corner and smiled. "Got those case notes for you. Hi, Bri."

"Courtney." Brianna stuffed her gloveless hands into her pockets and did a backward march to the exit. She lifted those startling blue and anxious eyes to me. "Come over tonight. About seven? I'll fix dinner."

Then she was gone. Courtney leaned up against the wall, her long wool military-style trench coat and black combat boots making her look like a pixie playing dress-up. She raised her eyebrows at Brianna's departure.

"Trying to pump you for info, is she?" Courtney stuffed her mittens in her knapsack purse and fished out a slightly soggy notebook. A lump of wet tissues fell out, landing with a soft plop on her right toe. "Want them now?'

"Come to my office," I said, picking up the tissues and handing them back to her. I gave a small wave to the room where Sean Farley waited more patiently than he ever had in life.

Courtney followed, tugging off her gear until, unbundled, she looked more like the forty-year old soccer mom she became when her investigative duties were finished for the day. I moved behind my desk. She dragged over a folding chair and flipped through her pages.

"Call came into the station at 1:57 a.m. regarding a light on in Compton's Jewelry. Pistol Pete was on duty."

We shared a grin. Pete Land fancied himself a detective. Courtney flipped the page. "When Pete went to investigate, he thought the store was locked. He used his flashlight to look through the grated windows and spotted a body lying on the floor. He tried the service door around back. It was unlocked, so he went in. The safe was open but he had no idea what, if anything, was missing. The body turned out to be a man wearing a ski mask. Land pulled the mask up and recognized Farley. He checked his vitals but got no pulse. He called the Life Squad, contacted the sheriff, called Mr. Compton, taped off the area."

"No obvious sign of a struggle? Weapons?" I doodled all our initials on my message pad. SF. PH. BC. AH. Four impossible sides of an old triangle locked together again. Fate.

Deja vu. Same old, same old.

"Nada. Only, this is strange. Land found a small empty glass container of olive oil, and a quart-size plastic water bottle, half empty, with the rest of the contents spilled all over the floor."

"Well, the autopsy will tell us what we need to know about Farley. Forensics'll deal with the plastic."

"Want me to observe?" Courtney closed her notebook.

"No," I told her, glancing out the window. "Type up those notes and leave them on my desk. Then take the rest of the day off. Weatherman says there's a storm moving in. At least three inches, maybe more."

Courtney raised her eyebrows at that. "You're giving me free time, boss? What's that all about?"

I waved off her amused grin. The phone rang.

"Hamilton Morgue," I said. "Harding."

Pete Land chattered at me, his voice level an octave above normal. Courtney could hear him from across the room.

"Doc," he shouted, "we got a fire. With fatalities."

"Where?"

He rattled off an address on Tilden Avenue. I jotted it down and tore the sheet off the pad.

"Dr. H?" Pete's voice snagged on my name. "It's bad. A woman, and two little kids."

"Need me?" Courtney asked.

I shook my head. "You've been burning a lot of midnight oil," I said, putting just the right note of sympathy into my delivery. "Go home. Relax. Spend some time with your kids."

Courtney cocked her head and pursed her lips. "If I didn't know better," she said, "I'd say you were trying to get rid of me. This have anything to do with your date tonight?"

I steered her out of my office and settled her at her desk. "It's not a date," I muttered. Her laughter followed me out the door.

Icy wet snow needled my forehead as I stepped outside the morgue and headed into the parking lot. Turtling into the collar of my jacket, I felt in my pockets for my gloves, but they were sitting on the dashboard of my car doing nobody any good. I jammed my hands in the pockets of my jeans. The left one ran up against the pre-paid cell phone I bought last week at Motley's Bargain Basement out by the interstate, and I thought about Farley and two quarts of water, remembering that old saying about hiding evidence in plain sight. By the time I reached the car, my bare cheeks stung and my fingers had started to cramp with cold. Right now, a fire sounded like a good idea. But that's a bit of morbid morgue humor. Like calling the changing area the Monica Room, after President Bill Clinton's tenure. Or writing *It's amazing how hard it is to find a lung* on the whiteboard in the autopsy room. When death's a constant companion, it's the living who give me the creeps.

✗　✗　✗　✗

In the twenty minutes it took to reach Tilden Avenue, the snow had picked up. Driven by a strong northwest wind, it covered the windshield faster than the wipers could clear it. I eased my way forward through the slick half-inch now covering the roadways and coating the singed bushes and trees around the Marberry cottage. Fire trucks lined the block, obstructing traffic. I pulled up behind a green Eco-Management trash truck out of Ross County. The driver, a short, bald, black man wearing a long-sleeved flannel shirt under a neon green caution vest, was standing by the driver's door, swearing and pounding his feet in frustration. I crunched my way over to the back of his truck. When he looked my way, I waved. Just before he reached me, I slipped the cell phone out of my pocket and dropped it into the trash piled up inside the bin, sending Farley's last phone call to me into oblivion.

"The wind's really picking up," I shouted. "Better close this or you'll have half of Hamilton's trash sailing out behind you."

"Shit, don't I know it," he sputtered, "but if I don't pick up the people's trash, the city gets calls and I get a reprimand."

I glanced toward the crime scene. The yellow tape strung around the front lawn of the house sagged already as the snow continued its assault. "Nothing's getting through here for hours. Best you move along."

He swallowed hard a few times, thinking about his supervisor, thinking about the man with the official ID badge pinned to the outside of his coat telling him to go away.

"You somebody important?" he asked.

I shrugged. "Just the coroner."

He stepped away, wiped his mouth and pulled the lever on the side of the truck. The bin door closed. We stared at each other, listening to Tilden Avenue's garbage compact itself inside the truck. Then he climbed back inside the cab and put the truck in gear. The beep-beep as he shifted into reverse blared at me. I shuffle-stepped my way to the sidewalk, putting Farley's final words and Brianna's invitation out of my mind and went to work. After all, that's what they pay me for.

✗ ✗ ✗ ✗

By six o'clock, the snow had layered itself into a neat three inches, the roof of the one-story stone and frame bungalow still smoked, and the fire chief had declared the site an arson investigation. The blaze itself had been confined to the kitchen at the back of the house, but the fire spread noxious fumes throughout the structure. After the firefighters brought the bodies out and laid them on the lawn, I did a cursory exam and closed the body bags up quickly. No mystery about the children. The smoke from the fire killed them while they slept. Besides, I hate to cut up kids. I called Anderson Funeral Home to come pick up the children.

The wife, Marissa Marberry, she was another story. Defensive wounds on her forearms, bruises all over her torso and legs. I looked over at Kenneth Marberry standing next to Pat's cruiser with his arms folded, biceps straining against the windbreaker he'd pulled on, and his sweatpants hanging low on his gym-hard hips, not shedding one damn tear. I sent a text to Bob Watson, telling him to take Marissa's body to the morgue. Then I stripped off my protective rubber gloves and checked my watch. It was already half past six. Brianna would be expecting me. Just before I reached my car, Pat reached me.

"Alan." He grabbed my arm. "You call Farley Tuesday night?"

"Do you believe that bastard Marberry?" I said, nodding back at the crime scene and blinking the snow off my eyelashes.

"Did you?"

I jerked my arm but his hand clamped tighter. I flexed my fingers three or four times. He got the hint. Releasing his grip, he moved closer, his boots crunching against the snow.

"I know you and he talked. A lot. What were you two planning?"

I leaned back on the fender of my Navigator. Pat took off his glasses, the lenses clouded now with wet, white flakes. "He say anything about robbing Compton's?"

I looked back at the Marberry house, then stared straight at him. "Yeah, Pat, he talked about it all the time. Dumb son-of-a-bitch. I told him it couldn't be done."

Pat pinched the bridge of his nose with one gloved hand and stared back. I jabbed at his chest with one frozen finger. "I didn't believe him."

"But you talked to him," he said, rubbing his hands together and stamping his feet.

"You talked to him, too."

Pat had the grace to look sheepish.

"Look," I said, "Farley just wanted to rehash old times. Since he got out of the Army, he had a hard time reconnecting. Especially after he couldn't get Brianna back." I made a sad face.

"So all you did was talk?"

"Yeah, Pat, same as you. And we never got further than the fight. How far did you get?" I pushed the remote to unlock the driver's door as I watched the memory of that last game of our senior year creep over Pat. I knew he was reliving the final rupture of our once-tight fraternity. And I went there with him. Recalled Farley and me scuffling and cursing and accusing each other of wanting Brianna. It was snowing that night, too, when I found her crying outside the locker room and gathered her up like a fallen angel. Then Pat came out and shouted that I was making a move on Sean's girl and Sean's fist slammed into me. A year later, Pat made his own move. Cut me and Farley out of the equation.

"Yeah, but what was he doing at the jewelry store? With oil and water and a cell phone? I can't see how it all fits."

"Well," I brushed snow off the windshield. My hand shook. "That was never your strong suit, was it?"

"Alan, you're a real prick."

I climbed into the Navigator. The engine stuttered and cranked on. "I guess that makes us a matched pair," I said. I slammed the door, leaving Pat with his mouth open and his eyes squinted shut and the white stuff tugging at his boots like an anchor.

⚔   ⚔   ⚔   ⚔

I pulled into the parking lot behind the yellow brick city building just as Watson arrived with Marissa Marberry's body. I waited in my car while he wheeled the gurney through the door and onto the scale. Then I checked my watch, ignored the anxious growl of my stomach and went inside.

"Evening, boss." Watson nodded at my muffled head. I unwound my scarf and tugged off my gloves. "Where you want this one?"

"Put her in the cold box," I said. "I have an appointment. I'll do her and Farley later. You know…"

He handed me a copy of the crime scene statements and finished my sentence. "Where there's no hope, there's no hurry. I hear ya, boss. You want me to stay?"

I moved to the window and shook my head. "Nothing but an accident waiting to happen out there. You go on home."

Watson shrugged. "Your place, your call. I'm as close as my phone."

I helped him roll Marissa's body in next to Farley's, clapped him on the shoulder as he left and checked the notes he'd given me. Kenneth Marberry's brief statement scrawled in block print over the lined statement pad. I scanned the time and date particulars, pausing to read the final quote. *She was planning to leave me. She was taking my children. I loved her.*

✗   ✗   ✗   ✗

The drive to Brianna's place, usually a quick twenty minutes, took over an hour. Thick drifts of snow had piled up around stop signs and mailboxes, obscuring the familiar landmarks. Doog's Deli, where Pat, Farley, and I hung out after practices. Malabar Cleaners, my first part-time job. The high school and stadium, dark and silent and somehow accusing. I inched the Navigator forward through the thick snow cover, parked a block away from Brianna's two-bedroom rental cottage on Foliage Lane and walked back through the alley. I saw lights on in the kitchen but chose to go around front. If anyone were watching, I didn't want to look like a thief. Right before I pressed the doorbell, I heard the heavy metal music ricocheting around the inside of the house. Brianna, ever the headbanger. I figured she wouldn't hear the ring, so I tried the latch. It was open.

Inside, the house smelled like gingerbread and stew. I dumped my boots on the floor mat and slid across the oak-paneled floor on my stockinged feet, faking a microphone in one hand and a beer in the other. Bri looked up from the stove. She laughed at me and for that one instant, we were best friends again. Closer than lovers. Free from the past. I stared a little too long and the frown came back and then I was just Doctor Alan Harding with the unenviable job of cutting up dead people, good old just-a-friend Alan, who might help her understand why Sean Farley died.

Spoon in hand, dark brown gravy dripping across the polished floorboards, Brianna hurried to the stereo and turned down the volume. She used her free hand to brush at the wisps of rich auburn hair that wandered across her face. "Dinner's not quite ready. Take a load off."

I shrugged out of my jacket and surrendered to the recliner, sighing as the leather curved around my back. One minute, I promised myself. I'd allow one minute without thinking about Farley lying on the slab and Pat puzzling over the robbery and Brianna trying to seduce me out of details. I nodded off.

⚬   ⚬   ⚬   ⚬

Brianna's insistent shaking woke me. She pulled up an ottoman and sat at the foot of the recliner, cell phone in hand, Farley's last message pulled up on the screen. I searched for a diversion.

"So, you've been waiting a long time, Bri." Thirteen years, to be precise. I did the math. "When are you and Pat tying the knot?"

Her face froze but her eyes strayed into unease. She glanced at her left hand. "Until we can afford to do things right, Pat says. Maybe next year. But now, the ring's gone—"

I leaned forward. "Okay. But money isn't everything. You deserve that family you always wanted. Remember?" And I watched yesterday steal over her. A minute passed and then Brianna Campbell let the memories go.

"Tell me, Alan," she said. "Please."

I considered leaving then, but I could smell her perfume, the same one she'd used all those years ago. "You first."

"I talked to Pete."

That made me angry. "Pete Land has no business discussing this with anyone."

"Well, he did." She looked down, drew a series of circles on the knee of her jeans, glanced back at me. "They tracked Sean's last phone call. It came from the city building."

"So." I had practiced this response. "What does that mean?"

"It means," she leaned forward, put one hand on my leg, "someone from the police station called him."

"Who was on duty?" I traced the outline of the armrest with one finger, trying to ignore the heat from her touch. "Bri?" I tried not to sound too eager.

She stood and paced the room, then rested one arm on the fireplace mantel and cleared her throat. "Pat. I think it was Pat."

"Well," I tried to sound firm, reassuring, "Pat could have any number of reasons to call Farley. But not in the middle of the night. You can forget about that." But I knew she couldn't, wouldn't. She chewed on a fingernail.

"You don't think Pat?"

"No." I got up and joined her in front of the fire. I slipped one arm around her shoulder and she leaned against me and I knew this was the best it would ever be between us. One minute of absolute comfort. Her body settled next to mine, a hiccup of content escaping like steam from an empty pot. I watched the pulse in her neck pump in and out, moved my thumb along the vein. So easy to caress. So easy to sever. I wondered if Kenneth Marberry had faced the same choice.

"If it wasn't Pat," she said, "was it you?"

I felt like a teenager caught in a game of truth or dare. Brianna wouldn't let this go.

I had to tell her something. Through the gauzy white curtains of the front window I watched a bubble of red light firm and fade. Bri's head turned toward the gleam and her eyes brightened with hope, suspicion warring with desire. I stepped away, touched her cheek, and let her go. Grabbing for my coat and boots, I headed toward the back of the house as I pulled them on.

"Your boyfriend's here. Time to go." I lifted my chin toward the window and the cop car pulling in along the curb.

"Wait, Alan. We can all talk about it."

I had almost reached the back door when she came at me, arms outstretched, panic driving her.

"Call me. When you finish the autopsy." She grabbed my shoulder and tried to spin me around. "Tell me what you find. I need to know how Sean died."

"Sure," I said, but I didn't mean it. Not one word. I slipped down the back steps and floundered along the walkway to the alley. "I'll let you know." And then I was gone, muddling through the snow, back to the car with Brianna's pleas and Farley's final question ringing in my ear. *Should I take the necklace*?

✗   ✗   ✗   ✗

The red caution light above the morgue entry door blinked at the blowing snow. I shuffled around the parked hearse, the radio warning of a level two snow emergency still ringing in my head. The county was essentially on lockdown. No one would come out tonight unless they had to. No big deal. The autopsies were mine to do, anyway, and I preferred to be alone.

I rolled Marissa Marberry's body into room one. Courtney, bless her, had set out all the instruments, the specimen slides, and a viscera bag for each body. In the Monica Room, I changed into my scrubs, slipped on my old comfortable pair of moccasins and went through my mental checklist of procedures. Back in the autopsy room, I switched on the CD player. A symphonic arrangement of *Sympathy for the Devil* filled the space.

When I unzipped the bag covering Marissa Marberry's body, I saw the marks around her neck. I lifted her head, noted the pressure point bruises behind the ears. Marissa's eyes, once a clear and eager violet, revealed the telltale petechiae. I didn't even need to look for the same fine red dots in her internal organs, but they were there. Kenneth Marberry didn't just strangle his wife. He obliterated her, crushing her airway and holding on until she was well and truly gone.

I took tissue samples, placed the internal organs in the bag and settled it back inside her abdomen. Then I finished dictating and stripped off my gloves. Mrs. Marberry lay on the table robbed of all her possibilities, not even a wedding ring to grace her swollen fingers. Her husband's rage killed her. That unreasoning descent into jealousy and a thirst for revenge. Uncontrollable anger for slights, real or imagined. Stupid, stupid, stupid.

By the time I stripped off my soiled clothing, my hands were shaking. I pulled on a fresh set of scrubs and hosed down the floor.

I rolled Marissa back to the cold box. Then I moved Farley down the hall to room two, checked the instrument table and clipped a microphone to the front of my shirt. "Here we are again," I whispered, uncovering his body, "you, me, and all the sins of our past. Bet you thought I'd be the first one on the table, didn't you?" Farley declined to answer. I thumbed on the recorder. *Weight: 180. Height: six-two. A thin white scar on the upper left shoulder from rotator cuff surgery. A pucker scar on his right hip from a bullet wound, another below the right clavicle, a series of cluster scars on the right thigh, souvenirs of the Iraq War.* I picked up the scalpel and began the Y incision, talking as I cut. Lifting, weighing, taking lung samples for histology to evaluate, but I knew what killed him.

When I slit open Farley's trachea, the necklace, eight medium-size rubies separated by small gold beads on an eighteen-inch chain, lay coiled up inside his airway. I took a digital photo, lifted it out and placed it on the scale. The stones were the actual trigger of death, closing off his breathing and causing him to suffocate, but Farley died from something more profound. Greed killed him, greed and desire and an untimely trust in the one person he shouldn't have trusted.

As soon as the official business was concluded, I clicked off the recorder and, just to be safe, unplugged the machine. No sense in messing up now. And I started over, Farley's last call cycling through my head. *The diamonds are bagged and swallowed. Should I take the necklace?*

I slipped the rubies into an evidence envelope and returned to an examination of Farley's stomach. The six small gray bags were there, tied with satin ribbon, as smooth and slippery as the oil floating in the water he used to wash them down. I lifted them out, rinsed them in alcohol and set them to dry on a towel. Then I stitched Farley back up and returned him to the freezer, wondering which of the stolen diamonds Pat had intended to give to Bri. When I looked up, I could swear I saw the ghost of Marissa Marberry hovering in the corner, the bruises on her neck fainter than the bruises on her soul.

Shaking off the vision, I rehearsed the next scene. *Walk to Pat's office.* Check. *Replace his answering machine tape with the one I made of Farley's final voice contact with me*. Check. I hurried to the Monica Room to change, came back for Farley's body. What had I forgotten? The envelope. I shoved it in my pocket and wrapped the diamonds up in the towel. They burned in my hand. I reached to switch off the overhead lights and Marissa's ghost drifted forward. I couldn't shake the feeling she was disappointed in me. Did I have this whole scheme figured wrong?

Farley's death. I hadn't counted on that and, technically, I couldn't be blamed. I told him it was a stupid plan, and I didn't choke him myself. But I could be held as an accessory. *If* they found out we'd planned to meet after he passed the stones, that we intended to divide the diamonds and go our separate ways. Simple enough to resolve our past differences, celebrate beating the odds and, after a suitable length of time, dust off the town and each other for good. Still, his demise had worked to my advantage, and, to be fair, I knew he couldn't swallow those rubies. I knew. Planting that ugly seed of suspicion in Brianna, now, that was all on me. Planting a fake tape in Pat's office, that was on my head, too. I blinked and Marissa's ghost shimmered away.

⚹   ⚹   ⚹   ⚹

In my office, I opened the safe and stashed the evidence envelope along with the autopsy tapes for Marberry and Farley. Then I spread out the towel and emptied the bags. The diamonds spilled out across the desktop. Under the light of the lamp, they sparkled like the freedom they represented, their brilliance a counterpoint to the heartache of the past. A million bucks worth of revenge. Living the *vida loca* in Mexico. Pat under suspicion and Brianna unmarried and alone and Farley nothing but a dead guy with a marker in the cemetery.

Using tweezers, I separated out one of the larger stones, a marquis cut perfect for an engagement ring. I lifted the diamond and studied its color. Then I slipped it into a small, padded mailer and sealed the flap. I used a green pen from Courtney's desk to fill out the address lines. My hand only shook when I printed Brianna's name. Someday I'd mail it.

I returned the gems to the bags and, holding them out like an offering, started down the hall, wondering which of Pat's files to hide them in. Halfway to his door, I just stopped walking. In the one-way pebbled glass door that separated the sheriff's quarters from the morgue, my reflection wavered at me. Alan Harding, a taller, less-muscular version of Kenneth Marberry, gloating. The image of Marissa Marberry's battered face, her ringless hands, superimposed itself over mine. The prospect of revenge got all swallowed up in her bloodshot eyes. I listened to the tick of an invisible clock and Farley telling me this was the best chance we'd ever have to pay them back. I moved back to the window in my office and noticed how the snow had distorted the landscape, wiping out the oil stains on the parking lot, covering the lines that told you where to park. All the old familiar markers had disappeared.

I started back toward Pat's office again, but I just couldn't take one more step. I thought about me and Farley jogging together, going around and around the same old track. I thought about asking Pat how many times he and Farley hashed over our same tired story, how far they got before they ran out of breath and excuses. I thought about Brianna drifting between the two of them, using me as an anchor whenever they disappointed her. And I thought about who I was, really, and who I wanted to be. Then I turned and headed back to the cold box. I wanted to run, but there was no need. Where there's no hope, there's no hurry.

It didn't take long to sew the diamonds inside Marissa. I imagined them moored there, a hundred tiny ships of light illuminating her corpse from within. After I washed up, I laced on my sneakers, grabbed my coat and headed into the storm.

✗

J.E. Irvin's stories have appeared in both print and online journals and magazines, including *Alfred Hitchcock Mystery Magazine* and *Spark a creative anthology*. Her award-winning debut novel, *Dark End of the Rainbow*, is available from the publisher, AbsolutelyAmazing eBooks, Amazon and Barnes & Noble.

LETTER OF THE LAW

by J. P. Seewald

"**I**f you're trying to prove you're a poor man's Sam Spade, I've got a flash for you, kid. Your imitation sucks." My old man's words were sharp as an ice pick and just as cold.

"Don't plan on giving a course in P.R. any time soon, Pop," I said.

"Tom's office will look better once it's decorated," my mother said, offering a faint smile.

In all fairness, my office did look a tad stark. The blue wallpaper had faded and peeled. Someone had ground chewing gum into the worn grey carpet. Two battered wooden desks and shabby chairs were left behind by the previous tenant. A single narrow window permitted a view of a brick wall and a dirty alley.

"Nothing short of a bomb blast will help this place," the old man said.

"It'll look better after a couple of beers. Let's go. I'm buying."

"With what?"

He had a point there, but I wasn't going to concede it. "I still have a few bucks in my pocket."

"I'm going to paint some landscapes for you," Mom said. "I'll do one to cover that crack in the wall." She pointed and I winced. "Maybe that picture I did of the Alps might be suitable. Blue and white, very soothing."

"That would be great," I said, trying to sound enthused.

I shut off the light switch in my office and locked the door—though I don't know why I bothered, since there was nothing worth stealing inside.

"So you still believe you did the right thing quitting your job and opening your own law office?" The old man's blue eyes zeroed in on me like kamikaze radar.

"I think I can make it work," I said.

"Thinking isn't knowing." Pop gave me one of his stern be-a-man looks.

"My job was a dead-end. I'm not sorry I left. I only signed a one year lease on the office. If I can't make a go of it, I'll look for another job when the lease runs out." That would be on my thirtieth birthday. So I'd have something to either celebrate or cry over. I planned to knock back a few on that day regardless.

"Stop being so down on the boy, John."

"He's not a boy. You should stop treating him like one."

I sighed. Since I can remember my folks have been arguing about me one way or another.

"Meantime, he's moving back with us like he was a kid."

My father frowned at me. At sixty-three, he wasn't aging well. His gut sagged over his belt and light tap-danced on his balding dome.

"It's only for the one year, so he can afford to pay his office rent," Mom said.

"Yeah, maybe. What kind of client is going to want to walk into a law office that looks like an armpit? Answer me that?"

"We'll fix it up," Mom said reassuringly.

"*We're* not going to do anything. That's his job." With that the old man stalked away toward the elevator.

"The office is in a good location," I called after him, "right near the courts." Why did I feel it was necessary to defend myself? Old habits die hard I guess.

"Don't worry, Tom, it's going to be all right," Mom said.

We joined the old man and waited for the elevator together in silence. When we reached ground level, my father turned to me again.

"Any idea how many ambulance chasers there are in the state of New Jersey?" Since it was a rhetorical question, I didn't bother offering an answer.

✗　✗　✗　✗

The next day, the phone rang only twice—a wrong number and someone soliciting. I got really sick of sitting at my desk and staring at the ugly wallpaper and carpeting. At five p.m., I walked over to Finnegan's Bar, where Happy Hour includes free food. A bunch of lawyers hung out there and I did a little networking since the place is like a New Jersey version of Cheers.

I arrived home around nine p.m. Mom smoothed her hands over her ample hips. "I replied to an ad for you in the *Ledger*. The man called today. He says he needs an attorney for his business. I took his number for you." She reached into the pocket of her stretch pants and pulled out a crumpled slip of paper.

I was going to tell her I doubted it would amount to anything, that lawyers didn't do business that way, but I didn't want to ruin her good mood. So I thanked her, took the paper and said I'd call the guy the following day.

✗   ✗   ✗   ✗

Derrick Banard had a clipped British accent with a slight musical quality. We talked for a while on the phone and I asked him some questions. It seemed he did indeed need an attorney to represent him in a number of litigations. He ran an insurance agency.

"I am a very busy man," he said. "Perhaps you might come by my office?"

I readily agreed, not exactly eager for him to see my office set-up. As it turned out, his office wasn't so fancy either. He did have two secretaries, one that looked like a biker chick, the other, definitely somebody's grandmother—maybe his.

Mr. Banard didn't keep me waiting very long, which I took as a good sign. In his mid-forties, he had sharp, hazel eyes, a pale complexion, and slicked-back hair. His suit looked like Armani. His shirt also appeared expensive, as did his gold cufflinks. His watch was a Rolex or a first-rate fake.

"Good to meet you," he said in that clipped accent. "Your secretary said you just opened your own office and were taking on new clients. I like enterprising young men." I didn't bother to tell him he'd confused my mother for a legal assistant.

Just as he'd stated, he had plenty of litigation connected to his insurance business. Even if I only had him for a client, I figured this guy could keep me busy for a while. There was one catch as I soon discovered, he wasn't willing to pay much. He expected strictly bargain rates.

"No attorney works for what you're willing to pay," I told him bluntly.

"But as you are just starting," he said with an oily smile, "I expect you will give me special consideration. I will in turn introduce you to some of my clients. Many of them are doctors."

Ka-ching!

"Of course, I will first have to see that your work for me is worthy."

This was not sounding so great, but I was in no position to bargain and the guy knew it. So I agreed to his sweat shop terms.

✗   ✗   ✗   ✗

One morning, I walked over to the university library which wasn't far from my office, to do some research on case law.

I was doing pretty well, finding the information I needed on the computer databases when an attractive young woman sat down next to me. Unaware of my incredible sex appeal and charm, she immediately began working. I wanted to do the same but found myself staring at her. A few times she looked up and we exchanged glances.

She had nice features, small pert nose, generous lips, dark, bright eyes, long straight black hair that hung past her shoulders. Her skin was flawless. When she finally stood up to leave, I found myself doing the same. She was slim and almost as tall as I was.

"Join me for a cup of coffee?"

She looked surprised, and then smiled. She had nice even teeth, too. "All right," she said. There was the hint of a foreign accent.

"Grad student?"

"Yes, how did you know?"

"You have the look."

"A courteous way to say I appear older than the undergraduates." She smiled again. "But you are not a student."

"Not any longer. I'm a lawyer."

She nodded her head. "I am impressed."

"Don't be. I'm just starting out on my own and it's a struggle."

She turned her head to one side in a gesture of appraisal. "You don't like working for other people?"

"I'd rather be my own boss."

"But then who will you have to blame if things go wrong?"

I shrugged. She did have a point and it wasn't on the top of her head. "So what are you studying?"

"You wish to change the subject." She gave me a knowing look.

"I must be transparent."

"Like a window pane," she agreed.

"I'd rather talk about you than me. I'm kind of a dull dude."

"I do not believe that." The appraising look was back again. "I have found that most men like to talk about themselves."

"You some kind of psychologist?"

When she smiled this time, a fetching dimple formed in her right cheek. "Yes, I am here for a degree in clinical psychology. I have a fellowship."

"So where are you from?"

"Chile."

"No kidding. I never met anyone from Chile before."

"It's a beautiful country. I think you would like it."

"Well, this is a big country. Hope you like it here." I took her slender hand in mine and shook it firmly. "My name's Tom Atkins, and you are?"

"Lara Lopez."

Over coffee at the student center, we talked. She was well-mannered and clearly well-bred.

"You really can speak four different languages? I barely manage English."

She laughed lightly. It was a good sound, like soft music.

"Were you studying psychology in your country?"

"I finished the program there and was working for several years. I was a prison psychologist."

I choked on my coffee, staring at her. "You're joking, right?"

She shook her head.

"Didn't your family object?"

There were shadows in her eyes. "I have no family, at least no close relations. I was orphaned as a child by an earthquake that destroyed our mountain village. Enough about me. Tell me about yourself."

"I was more interested in sports than studying back in school."

"What sort of sports?"

"Football, wrestling, baseball. After high school, I joined the Marines. Did a tour of duty, but the military wasn't the right career for me. I'm not great at taking orders from other people. So I went to college, studied accounting, but decided crunching numbers wasn't for me either. That's when I figured I'd give law school a try."

"Is your father also a lawyer?"

"Pop? No way. He was in construction until he was forced to retire. Injured his back in a scaffolding accident."

"That is terrible. Is he better now?"

"He lives on painkillers."

"I am sorry for his suffering."

"Don't be. He makes other people suffer right along with him."

After we finished polishing off a second cup of coffee, I took her to see my office, an act of total insanity.

She looked around, wide-eyed. At first, she was silent. Then she turned and studied me for what seemed an eternity. "You need my help," she said, biting her lower lip.

"Do I?"

"Most certainly. I will work part-time as your assistant."

"I can hardly pay the rent, much less pay your salary."

"You can't afford not to hire me," she asserted.

"Wouldn't working here interfere with your studies?"

"No, I am an A student. It's not a problem for me."

Just like that, it was settled. Lara was going to be my assistant. And I'd pay her what I could. Truth was I really did need someone to help me out. Organization was never my strong point. And she would definitely improve the appearance of the office.

✗   ✗   ✗   ✗

A few days later, I got a phone call from Mr. Banard.

"I have a client for you," he said without preamble.

"Did you give him my phone number?"

"This is not an ordinary client." It seemed that my question had somehow offended him.

"I consider all my clients special," I said. I had too few of them to do otherwise.

"You do not understand. This man has dined with world leaders. Unfortunately, Dr. Sarder has fallen on hard times. Still, you must accord him the utmost respect."

I took down the information Mr. Banard gave me, which was sketchy at best.

"You must be willing to meet Dr. Sarder at his office. He expects this courtesy."

"I'm willing to meet the client at his office," I affirmed.

Banard said that he'd get back to me and hung up.

Lara was listening to my end of the conversation. When I got off the phone, she turned to me, a frown of disapproval in evidence on her lovely face. "This is not good. Your clients should always come to *your* office. It is not professional for you to go to them."

"Yeah, I know, but this place is kind of a dump. It's not going to impress these guys."

"Well, I am going to help you fix it up," she said with an air of determination. "I was planning to mention it to you, but I did not wish to offend you. However, now you have brought it up yourself. I know ways to improve this office."

I didn't doubt her. There was a sparkle in those bright eyes that told me she was assessing the place with the eye of an interior decorator, a regular Martha Stewart.

During the next week, ivy plants and attractive prints started appearing as if by magic. A bookcase, used but in good condition, was delivered to the office. My files and books were neatly organized. The place was clean. Curtains appeared on the window.

As I came in one morning, slightly hung over from wooing clients at Finnegan's Bar the previous evening, Lara was already there working on the files, making efficient noises. I groaned inwardly. She took one look at me and produced a cup of coffee. I blinked. Where had the coffee maker come from? I sniffed the air. Cinnamon buns. God, I love cinnamon buns! But I knew in the interest of fairness, I had to say something.

"Lara, where did all this stuff come from? I'm not paying you enough."

She shrugged. "You needed some things. I have a little money."

"Thanks," I said. "Everything you've done is terrific. But give me the receipts for what you spent and I'll repay you. You should be spending your money on yourself, not on me. And I do appreciate your efforts, especially the coffee."

"It will be good for your clients. When they come in, they will smell fresh coffee. It will be welcoming."

"Yeah, but for what clients?"

She smiled, the cute dimple forming in her right cheek. "There will be clients. I have faith in you."

Which was more than I had. But I kept my mouth shut on the subject. As if in response to Lara's affirmation, the phone rang.

Lara answered the phone in a professional voice. "I will see if he is available. Please hold." She turned to me. "It's Mr. Banard."

I nodded and switched desks with her. "Tom Atkins here."

"Will you be available to meet Dr. Sarder this afternoon?"

"I can manage to fit him in," I said, hoping my eagerness wasn't too obvious.

✗ ✗ ✗ ✗

Seated beside Banard in the backseat of his Mercedes as his driver whisked us down for our initial meeting, I got filled in on the doctor's background.

"Arthur is in straitened circumstances. He has many financial problems. Creditors are attacking him and his partner on all fronts. He can no longer pay the top attorneys he has been accustomed to employing in the past. You may be of service to him. But you must show him proper respect."

"Sure, just don't expect groveling." Which was one reason I no longer worked at my previous job, but I wasn't about to go into that with Banard.

Dr. Sarder wasn't quite what I expected. For one thing, he was a chain smoker. This would not have been so surprising if Mr. Banard hadn't told me that Dr. Sarder was a cardiologist by profession. From the moment I laid eyes on Dr. Sarder, it was clear to me that he was not in good health. His skin had a sallow cast to it. I figured his age around sixty, maybe a year or two younger than my old man.

Sitting beside the good doctor was an attractive woman, not young but well-maintained. Her hair was a brassy blond, her blue eyes sharp and assessing. She wore a white designer suit and carried herself like a queen.

After the basic intros, the grilling began. Dr. Sarder and his partner, Kala Thaler, began asking me questions. Of the two, she was the more incisive inquisitor. After a while, her teeth began to give the illusion of fangs and I swear she was ready to suck out my blood. My hand went instinctively to my jugular, as if I needed to convince myself it was intact.

"Are you the graduate of an Ivy League law school?" she asked.

"Nope." They both stared at me as if I'd told them I was an alien.

"Mr. Atkins formerly worked for a large New York City law firm," Banard quickly said. That seemed to thaw the chill some, but it was still mighty cold in the room.

I decided it was time for me to start asking questions. "Dr. Sarder, what sort of legal services are you seeking?"

He and Kala exchanged looks which I was in no way able to read. Then he cleared his throat. "My partner and I owned a group of nursing homes throughout the state, but most particularly in Northern New Jersey. We did well until the political climate changed. Now we are accused of providing inadequate care to our patients. It is not true, but that hardly matters. We find ourselves faced with bankruptcy. I have an attorney who specializes in bankruptcy to handle our financial problems. However, I had a contract with a very influential and important man in North Jersey. I was assured that if I paid him one million dollars as a consulting fee, there would be no more problems of any kind. Clearly, that was not the case. I would like to hire an attorney who is not afraid to sue this man."

"Just who is this person?"

The doctor lit a cigarette, inhaled deeply, and then began to speak again. "His name is Kevin Connolly."

I let out a low whistle. "The kingmaker?"

Dr. Sarder nodded his assent. "Precisely."

"Well, it won't be easy, but I'll do it for you."

"You are not frightened?"

"I'm not easily frightened." I eyed Sarder with a steady gaze.

He in turn exchanged a look with his partner who gave him an imperceptible nod.

"How much money will you require?"

"A case like this will require depositions and that gets expensive. I'll need five thousand up front and I'll work it off at an hourly wage."

"We cannot afford that in our present situation," Kala said, rising to her feet.

"Well, what can you afford?"

"I will offer you one thousand dollars," Dr. Sarder said.

"Make it two," I said, feeling like someone haggling at a third world bazaar. "There's going to be a lot of paper work and filings."

"Fifteen hundred dollars," Kala said. "And you will be paid in cash."

It left a bad taste in my mouth but I shrugged my agreement. "That'll be about enough to get started. I'll draw up a retainer agreement for both of you to sign. I'll also need access to all the documents related to your agreement with Connolly."

"Our secretary will help you." Kala led me through to the older woman who acted at both secretary and receptionist.

✗   ✗   ✗   ✗

"**Y**ou did well," Banard said to me on the drive back to New Brunswick. "They were impressed by you."

"I think they were more interested in the fact that I'd work dirt cheap."

"I vouched for your ability and integrity," Banard said. "They trust my judgment."

I wasn't so sure I did, but I kept that thought to myself.

Banard deigned to visit my office for the first time. His initial reaction was to raise his nose as if he smelled something unpleasant. Too bad Lara wasn't there with fresh coffee brewing.

We settled in and Banard told me how he was being sued by several individuals and needed me to represent him. "If you continue to work for me at the same rate, I'll find you more clients," he said.

Soon after he left, I got another phone call. I let the machine pick it up. I was also learning to screen my calls because the phone rang fairly frequently now, but most of the people calling had frivolous lawsuits at best that weren't worth any attorney's time and effort.

Lara came in around six p.m. while I was still poring over Dr. Sarder's legal papers. The contract with Kevin Connolly was straightforward. It stated that he was to be paid one million dollars for his consulting services. Said services were defined as promoting Dr. Sarder's nursing homes and medical clinics with people of influence and finding investors for said businesses should this become necessary. Dr. Sarder had stated that Connolly took the money but provided no services in return.

Taking on Connolly, one of the most powerful men in the state, was going to be far from easy. For one thing, no judge in his or her right mind would rule against the guy, not in North Jersey anyway.

"Why are you frowning so?" Lara asked.

"Was I?"

"Yes, deep frowning. It will make you look older than your years."

"I got more to worry about than that."

She raised her elegant dark brows.

"I've agreed to take a case for one of Mr. Banard's friends."

"Will he pay you?"

"Yeah, he'll pay."

Lara offered a smile. "Isn't that good?"

"It is and it isn't. The guy I need to sue for him is powerful."

She urged me to explain the situation to her.

"The thing is, this Connolly character has strong political connections. His support in North Jersey makes or breaks candidates. He's a power broker. They call him the Priest because he's austere, never been married, devotes himself completely to his career."

I went back to studying the documents in front of me. Even if Dr. Sarder and his partner still had a lot of money to throw around, it was unlikely that any established attorney would have taken on their case. It could be career suicide. Lucky for them I had very little to lose.

✗　✗　✗　✗

I met Dr. Sarder and Kala for depositions at the impressive offices of O'Neill, Norris, Weshell and Associates, a high-end law firm located in North Jersey.

We were pretty much treated like pond scum, left waiting for a full hour, totally ignored, without even so much as the offer of a cup of coffee or a glass of water. So much for common courtesy. The practitioners of civil law can be highly uncivil.

Dick Norris, dressed in designer duds, power tie, French cuffs, faced us with a frown. There was something distinctly lacking in the room, namely his client.

After the formalities were taken care of, we got down to business.

"Where's Kevin Connolly?" I asked.

"You expected him to come here today?"

"Well, yeah, I mean we did agree to depositions."

"For your clients. Mr. Connolly is in very poor health."

Dr. Sarder rose from his chair, face red as a rare roast. "This is an outrage. We refuse to be deposed if he won't."

Norris, cool as a glacier, shrugged his well-padded shoulders. "It's your lawsuit. It won't go forward unless you're deposed. Counselor, why don't you explain matters to your clients."

"I think you're stalling."

Norris stared at his manicured nails. "Mr. Connolly suffers from severe diabetes. He's almost blind. He's also got a serious heart condition. His physician says he could die at any time. You want to talk to his doctors? They'll verify what I'm telling you."

I groaned inwardly. Great, now I was harassing a dying man—if Norris was to be believed. "Can I depose Mr. Connolly at his home?"

"So long as your clients aren't present."

Norris set up the appointment and that was how I finally got to meet the great man himself at his estate. As I looked around, I considered that if all else failed, I could always put a lien on his mansion—provided the court agreed to enforce the contract. But I knew that wasn't likely. Dr. Sarder was really pursuing the matter more from injured pride. I realized there was little chance of his collecting.

I had already done quite a bit of research on Connolly. He claimed to be broke like Dr. Sarder, but the man had access to a great deal of money over the years, both legally and illegally. No doubt he had stashed plenty of cash out of the country.

I drove through iron gates, then drove slowly up a long, drive curving around grounds that were expertly maintained. A middle-aged woman who appeared to be a housekeeper greeted me at the door and led me across a marble foyer into a huge living room furnished with fine antiques. Norris was seated with Kevin Connolly. I had no trouble recognizing Connolly due to the dark glasses he wore. He had silver hair and a florid complexion. He was dressed casually in slacks and a flannel shirt.

There was no shaking of hands, no exchange of pleasantries. The legal stenographer was late in arriving. A tense silence gripped the room; it felt like a tomb. Connolly was inscrutable behind those dark glasses, his expression impossible to read. I decided that I ought to have brought Lara with me.

I glanced impatiently at my watch. "Mr. Connolly, why not offer to pay back some of Dr. Sarder's money? I'm certain we could come to an amicable agreement."

"Don't answer him," Norris instructed his client, "not until you're formally deposed."

Kevin Connolly inclined his head.

"Why can't we compromise?"

Norris rounded on me. "Listen, you green kid, those clients of yours are dishonest."

"And your client isn't?"

"This is a stupid waste of time. Your clients are going to withdraw their lawsuit. Hope you got your money upfront. You won't see another penny from them." He gave me a smug smile.

I figured this was just macho posturing. Dick Norris reminded me of a strutting rooster. Still, I admitted to feeling uneasy. It was as if he knew something I didn't.

⚹ ⚹ ⚹ ⚹

The following morning, Dr. Sarder phoned. He sounded shaky.

"Mr. Atkins, I have decided not to go ahead with my lawsuit. I do not wish to pursue the matter."

I wasn't sure what to think. "Mind telling me why?"

"Not over the telephone."

"You want me to come to your office?"

"No, I will visit yours."

We set up a time and I asked Lara to be present. I was completely baffled and wanted her input. But Sarder didn't show up for our meeting. When I phoned his office, his secretary said that he was unavailable.

"What do you think?" I asked Lara.

She was thoughtful, tapping a pencil for several seconds. "Did Dr. Sarder sound fearful?"

"I think he was frightened. I wonder if Connolly's attorney threatened him in some way."

"That would not be ethical for an attorney."

"Welcome to the real world."

"I thought America was different." Lara pushed back a lock of shiny black hair.

"Theory and practice are two different things."

"What will you do?"

I got up from my desk and started pacing the office. "What can I do? It's Sarder's decision. I hate to let it go, but that's his right, his call."

✗   ✗   ✗   ✗

We'd been working companionably for several hours and I was just about to suggest we break for dinner when the phone rang. Lara was working on a paper of her own that was due in a few days so I took the call myself.

"You must come right away!"

It took me a moment to place the voice. Dr. Sarder. Something had spooked him.

"What's wrong?"

"Mr. Connolly. He's dead."

"Not to sound insensitive, but how does that matter to you or me?"

I heard Sarder expel a breath. "The police are here. They want to question me. They are acting as if they think I murdered him."

"See you soon. In the meantime, refuse to answer any questions until I get there. Wise old saying: a fish can get hooked only if it opens its mouth." I turned to Lara. "Got time to pay a house call on a doctor?"

"Am I needed?"

"You could be."

Lara put her schoolwork away. We grabbed our coats and had the office locked up in a matter of minutes.

Dr. Sarder's house was in a nice suburban neighborhood. The house itself was not a development clone. It stood in solitary splendor and dignity at the rear of a cul-de-sac.

We were greeted at the door by a young woman who I took to be a maid. She led us into a spacious living room tastefully furnished.

No surprise, Dr. Sarder and Kala were seated on either end of a velvet couch like a pair of bookends. Two big men who had cop written all over them completed the tableau. Sarder looked relieved when I entered the room. Kala was wringing her hands. The younger of the two detectives was clicking a pen and flipping a small black notebook open.

"Gentlemen, Dr. Sarder isn't going to make any statement until he and I have a chance to talk."

If looks could kill, I would have keeled over.

The older detective cleared his throat. He had a face like a pit bull. "If your client's innocent, why does he need you? Why can't he answer our questions here and now?" The pit bull's eyes narrowed. At least he hadn't bared his teeth.

Instinctively, I knew there was no right answer to that question; so I had no intention of answering it. "Detective, maybe you could make an appointment to talk with my client at another time." I kept my tone of voice polite but firm.

"Fine," the older cop practically growled. Then he pulled a card from his jacket pocket and handed it to me.

I handed him one of my cards in exchange.

"I expect to hear from you tomorrow," he said in a gravelly voice that told me he was a serious smoker. He also smelled like a human ashtray.

I glanced down at his card. "I'll be in contact, Lieutenant Monroe."

"You better be."

The younger cop cast an appreciative eye over Lara. Then they took off.

Kala jumped up instantly. "So glad they're gone," she said. She turned to Sarder. "Is your chest hurting? Shall I have the girl bring your pills?"

"Just sit down," he said irritably. He turned toward me. "I need your legal expertise. Those policemen told me that Kevin Connolly was killed two nights ago. They say he was smothered in his sleep. They believe his attacker used a pillow which was pressed over his face, causing asphyxiation. His attorney told them that I threatened to kill Mr. Connolly."

"It is totally absurd," said Kala. "Anyone who knows Arthur can testify what a gentle man he is. Arthur is a doctor. He pledged to help the sick, not kill them." She savagely punched a sofa pillow. I got the feeling she was not so gentle-natured.

"I would never have murdered the man," Sarder said. "That does not mean I didn't wish him dead."

"You might have had a motive, but that doesn't prove you had the opportunity. Did you ever visit Connolly's home?"

"Never, only his office."

"Connolly was dying. It seems odd that someone would murder him. If it was one of his heirs, why not just wait? You want me to do some investigating on your behalf?"

"I do indeed, Mr. Atkins. These policemen acted as if I were guilty of murder. I'm afraid of what they will do to myself and to my family." Sarder's hands shook as he gestured, and I was reminded that he wasn't in such great health himself.

"Try not to worry. I'll find out everything I can about Connolly."

I wasn't about to say anything to them, but I'd seen cases like this before, where the police zero in on someone, deciding they were the guilty party and never really looking past that individual. If Sarder was the suspect they'd decided on, no question about it, he was in trouble, big time.

"Do you want me to find you a criminal attorney?"

"That would be a good idea," Kala said with a toss of her golden hair.

"And what will I pay him with?" Sarder gave her a hard look. "No, Mr. Atkins, you are a good liar. I trust you."

I hoped he meant that I was a good lawyer but decided not to press him. Sometimes it's better not to know what other people are thinking.

"I'll get started on this for you right away," I told him.

"Is this lovely young woman your assistant?" Dr. Sarder smiled for the first time.

"Yes, I am," Lara said, moving toward him. "And you are quite right to trust Mr. Atkins. He is an excellent attorney," she stated in a dignified manner that defied anyone to disagree.

"I like to gamble in Atlantic City, to shoot craps," Sarder said. "However, I can no longer afford to do so. But I am still a gambler at heart. I am betting on you. So roll the dice, Mr. Atkins, roll the dice for me."

We left them then, my mind already formulating a plan for handling the police, working on a stalling, delaying tactic.

"What do you think of them?" I asked Lara on the drive home.

She shrugged. "Your clients? I don't think either of them killed Mr. Connolly, but they do not strike me as the most reputable of people."

"You can tell on such short acquaintance?"

"I have instincts about people."

"Okay, I trust your judgment." And I did. However, being aware that Dr. Sarder and Kala weren't the most honest characters and probably would never tell me the whole truth, I couldn't help but feel discouraged.

I had a hunch this was going to be tough-going. I hoped I'd be up to it. I'd only done civil cases at my Manhattan firm, steady, staid corporate stuff. Criminal law was a whole new set of rules, a different world. But I supposed when you work for yourself, you have to be willing to take on any kind of case. Anything for a buck.

✗   ✗   ✗   ✗

Bright and early the next morning I was on the job. My office was freezing. The heat wasn't working. I found it hard to concentrate and called the custodian. I tipped him a few bucks, hoping he could get the old radiator to heat up.

He rubbed his Hitler mustache, looked at the ancient radiator dubiously and told me he'd see what he could do. "If I was you, I'd get a space heater as a back-up, just in case."

"I'll do that."

Sitting in my overcoat, I looked up the phone number of my old law school roommate, Bill Gerner. He was working for a small law firm in South Jersey that had a good database. I got through to him with more ease than expected. After disposing of the usual pleasantries, I got down to business.

"Bill, can you do some digging around for me on Kevin Connolly?"

"You mean the big-shot power-broker who just got himself whacked?"

"The very same."

"Why do you want to know about that guy?"

"Long story. I got a client who's involved."

"Let me guess, you want me to ask Karen to dig up info."

"If it wouldn't be too much trouble."

"You could just ask her directly."

"She'd turn me down."

"Okay, I'll do it for you, but you owe me a good lunch."

"You got it. Bring your information along with you."

Bill was dating Karen Jenkins, who'd graduated with us. The difference was that Karen was a demon of a worker and had graduated at the very top of our class. She'd gotten a number of offers but decided to work for the attorney general's office. That made her privy to a lot of important information. Bill could ask her for info. She'd go the extra mile for him.

Until I got that information, I wasn't going to allow the cops to interrogate Dr. Sarder. So I got back to them, told Lieutenant Monroe that my client was suffering chest palpitations, doubtless because of stress. I pointed out that the doctor suffered from a serious heart condition.

Then I took myself off to the university library to find out everything I could on my own. The Byzantine labyrinth of New Jersey politics wasn't all that easy to follow. But I forced myself to delve into the murky depths.

✗　✗　✗　✗

So what did Karen have to say?"

"Plenty. This better be a really good lunch." My old roommate stared at me through his dark-framed glasses that defined his eerily pale gray eyes.

"You're lucky I didn't take you to McD's. I'm that broke."

"Bull, I know you squirreled a few bucks away while you were working."

"You're a real pal," I said.

"Better than you deserve. So cut the sarcasm."

I let that pass. The waiter brought us our menus. We were sitting in a Chinese restaurant about a block away from my office building. The food was good here but not too expensive.

Bill ordered pot stickers as an appetizer and shrimp in lobster sauce as his entrée. We both took the hot and sour soup. I decided on shrimp with mixed vegetables and we both went for the fried rice.

Over cups of hot tea, I pressed Bill for information. He wasn't eager to spill, enjoying his advantage over me.

"So what does the A.G.'s office know about Connolly that could have gotten him murdered?"

"Don't know about getting him whacked, but he was in a lot of trouble. He was being investigated by the F.B.I."

"Do tell."

"Oh, I intend to. Think I'll have an order of spare ribs on the side."

I let out a deep sigh. He laughed, totally enjoying my irritation. "Here's what Karen found out. Guess who was going to wear a wire for the Feds?"

"Why would Connolly even consider doing it?"

"Because they had him. One of his pals gave him up, then went into the Witness Protection Program. Connolly wouldn't suffer the humiliation of going on trial."

"He was going to die soon anyway. Couldn't he just stall?"

Bill shrugged and slurped down the soup.

"Maybe he wasn't as sick as he made out. Could've been a bid for sympathy. He was a tough old bird."

"If you're right…"

"Hey, I'm always right. Besides, Karen's boss is in the know. He told her. She told me. Now I'm telling you."

"That means a lot of people could have wanted Connolly dead, people he might rat out."

"Yeah, word is he had something on just about everyone who was anyone. That includes wise guys."

"Like who?"

Bill merely smiled like a Cheshire cat with a bird in its sights. "Don't know, but I could probably find out. It'll cost you a better meal though. And this time it's Karen and me."

I agreed without hesitation. "Sure. I'd like to see Karen again."

"You just want to grill her like a hamburger. Don't try fooling an old friend, Tommy boy, I know you too well." Bill smirked at me. He had me at his mercy and he knew it. I kept my mouth shut.

Bill had given me a whole lot to chew on. Clearly, there was more to Connolly's death than was ever dreamed of in my narrow philosophy. Whoever killed him or ordered a hit on him might be someone mob connected. That didn't exactly thrill me. Dr. Sarder wasn't offering combat pay. In fact, he wasn't paying me much at all. But I was no coward. The Marine Corps had trained me to hang tough.

I marched back to the library and started digging for more information on Kevin Connolly and his family. He had no wife, no children, as I expected. But there was mention of a niece and nephew in the newspaper article I located. I went back to the office and looked up Dick Norris's phone number in the rolodex that Lara had so perfectly arranged for me.

I asked the receptionist to put me through to Norris, but she was no fool. She insisted on knowing who I was. I got as far as Norris's secretary and no further. It seemed Mr. Norris was with a client. When I phoned two hours later, he was out of the office. Not very original, but effective. I knew there wasn't much point in calling back again and asking to speak to Norris. But I did call back and ask when and where Kevin Connolly's funeral was being held. That information at least was given freely.

✗   ✗   ✗   ✗

There was a time when someone like Kevin Connolly would have had a funeral in the style of a potentate, but the service and subsequent burial had a limited number of people. He died under a cloud of suspicion.

At the funeral parlor, I went downstairs to the administrative office and inquired for information.

"I want to send fruit baskets and flowers to Mr. Connolly's family. Would you happen to have the names and addresses of his close relatives? I believe there's a niece and nephew."

The young man at the desk was hesitant, but I gave him my friendliest smile. "Mr. Connolly will be missed by his friends in the community," I said. "We want to show a token of our respect and esteem to his relatives."

That sold it. I got all the information I needed. I could have left and gone back to my office then, but I wanted to see who would show up at the cemetery. It wasn't hard picking out the niece and nephew. She was a solidly built woman in her middle to late thirties. The nephew had to be her brother. They didn't look much alike except in facial features. He was leaner, taller, and younger than she was. He had a ruddy complexion and black hair while she was a redhead with freckles. No one appeared particularly suspicious. No one wore a neon sign that said: *I killed Kevin Connolly.*

"So counselor, what are you doing here?" Dick Norris slithered up to me as Connolly was lowered into the ground.

"Same thing you are, paying my respects."

He gave me a crooked smile. "Somehow I doubt that."

"Maybe I was curious."

"Like a cat?"

"Could be," I agreed.

"Well, you know what happened to the cat."

"Yeah, he had nine lives." We were eyeball to eyeball.

"I was thinking more in terms of the old saying: curiosity killed the cat."

The redhead moved between us. "Dick, thanks for all your help. Gerald and I will make an appointment to sign the papers in a few days. We'd like to receive our inheritance as soon as possible, what there is of it, anyway." Connolly's niece gave Norris a wry smile.

He took her hand. "Certainly, Fiona, just give my secretary a call and we'll set up a meeting as soon as possible."

She moved on to join her brother and shake more hands.

"Well, I guess I know who inherits," I said.

"That's right," Norris agreed.

"Why did you sic the cops on my client?"

Norris bared his teeth. "Because I believe he had a reason to kill Kevin."

"Not like his heirs, who were maybe getting tired of waiting around for Connolly to kick off?"

"Get out of here! You don't belong here. You're a two-bit shyster who doesn't know the first thing about decent conduct."

Several people looked in our direction when Norris raised his voice, including Connolly's niece and nephew.

"I think you know a lot more about being a shyster than I ever will." I spoke in a soft, controlled voice. Then I turned on my heels and walked away.

✗   ✗   ✗   ✗

Lara and I met Karen and Bill in the waiting area of Duran's, a steakhouse renowned for serving slabs of quality beef. Karen and Lara hit it off immediately. That was a pleasant surprise. Karen had an aggressive personality. Lara seemed to understand that and didn't challenge her, radiating warmth. They had nothing in common from what I could tell, but it didn't seem to matter.

We took a table that looked out on the avenue. A waitress quickly came over to take our drink order. Lara requested cranberry juice while the rest of us ordered beer.

"Don't they drink in Chile?" Bill asked Lara.

"Of course, we do, but I do not like alcohol. I prefer water or juice."

Bill frowned at her. I could tell he was put out by this high-minded declaration. Bill tended to take the low road.

"Steaks are on me," I said.

Bill's mood immediately improved. We put away a good meal. And after Bill and Karen had a few more drinks, I felt the mood was relaxed enough for me to bring up Kevin Connolly. So I began by telling them a little about my client.

"I think the cops are trying to peg him for a crime that someone else committed. I'd really appreciate anything you can tell me."

Karen glanced around. "I don't know much, but I did find out that Connolly was going to roll over on Tony the Terrorist Alfonso. You've heard of him, right?"

"Who is this man?" Lara asked.

Karen ran her right hand through her short blond hair. "He's a made man, a gangster. He'd tell you he's a businessman, and he is.

But he runs as many illegal as legal enterprises. We've been trying to put the arm on him for years. The FBI is working on the case too. They pressured Connolly into helping them."

I straightened in my chair. "So would you say there's a chance Alfonso got wind of what was going on and eliminated Connolly?"

Karen bit her lower lip. Her dark blue eyes met my own directly. "It's possible. My boss thinks there could be a mole in our office. But Tom, this is strictly off the record. If anyone knew I was giving you this information, I'd be fired on the spot. My career would be over."

I nodded my head and quietly thanked her for what she had offered me.

"Just be really careful. These wise guys would put a hit out on you as soon as look at you."

✗   ✗   ✗   ✗

Police interrogation rooms are not pleasant places. This one was just what I expected. Dr. Sarder looked sick and miserable, his skin sallow and eyes shadowed. I could only hope he'd kept his mouth shut as I'd instructed him to do.

Lieutenant Monroe looked up as I entered the room. I noted the glass that indicated a two-way mirror and wondered who might be listening in on the other side.

"Your client isn't cooperating."

"That's because he's not supposed to talk to you unless I'm present, as you well know."

We faced each other like gunfighters at high noon, except I wasn't carrying a weapon.

"I was just asking your client where he was on the night Kevin Connolly died."

"He was with me," Kala interjected.

Monroe zeroed in on her, eyes narrowing into bullets.

"Just how can you be so certain?"

"We are together every evening." Her face heated with color.

Monroe stared at her. "If I'm buying that, then maybe you killed Connolly together."

Dr. Sarder rose to his feet, protesting. I placed my hand on his shoulder.

"That's a ridiculous accusation and you know it," I said.

"Maybe, maybe not. I need to fingerprint both of you," Monroe said, turning to Kala and Dr. Sarder.

"Are you arresting my clients? If so, on what evidence?"

"I thought only the Doc was your client."

I turned to Kala. "Can you give me a dollar?"

She nodded and fished in her purse, handing me a five dollar bill. I took the money and pocketed it.

"She's also my client now."

"Before we're done they'll be ratting each other out." He pointed to Kala with his index finger. "I'd advise you to get a separate mouthpiece."

"I have nothing to hide," she said, raising her chin.

Monroe shrugged with indifference. "Suit yourself. As for the fingerprinting, if you really have nothing to hide, then getting a little ink on your hands shouldn't be a problem."

I considered it a form of harassment. But since my clients didn't object, I didn't either. It might be one way of establishing that they hadn't been to Connolly's house. Of course, Monroe would probably just claim that they'd used gloves.

Before I left with my clients I decided to aim a parting shot at the police detective. "If you were really interested in investigating who murdered Kevin Connolly, you might have a talk with Tony Alphonso. I understand the FBI was planning to use Connolly to collect evidence against him. Given Alphonso's reputation, he might not have taken kindly to Connolly collaborating with the Feds."

Monroe's face turned scarlet. "What's your source of information?"

"It's common knowledge. See you around."

I got myself and my clients out of there quick as a jack rabbit.

⚹　⚹　⚹　⚹

Bill phoned my cell later in the day. "Just wanted to give you a heads-up on something. Your Kevin Connolly gets more interesting all the time."

"How so?"

"Karen says he had unnumbered Swiss bank accounts."

I was on full alert. "She sure?"

"Oh, yeah."

My brain clicked away. So Connolly's niece and nephew did have a motive for murder. Connolly squirreled away money, probably a lot of it. I decided to check out his heirs more closely, see if I could get info on their financial situations.

✗ ✗ ✗ ✗

I was thinking about it again the following day as I walked toward my office. Suddenly, two big men came around either side of me. I tried to cross to the other side of the street, but a black Lincoln with tinted glass windows cut in front, blocking my escape.

The car window at the back rolled down. "Get in, Atkins." The voice was gruff, with a New York accent.

"I think you got the wrong guy."

"No, we know who you are." The man speaking was middle-aged and heavy-set.

"My mother told me never to get into a car with strangers. Mother knows best."

The man seemed to find that amusing. "Is that right? Well, we're not strangers. You've been tossing my name around. So get in the car because we need to have a little discussion."

I'm not into being beaten to a pulp or worse, so I stood fast. I assumed I was talking with Tony the Terrorist. He nodded to his two goons.

The man who strikes the first blow is usually at an advantage, especially when it's not expected. I had some training in the military. I swung around and smashed the first guy hard in the gut. He bent over and began retching. The second man didn't spend more than a second looking surprised. He started reaching inside his jacket and I knew it wasn't for cough drops or cigarettes.

This guy looked like he'd boxed at one time or another. His nose was crooked, like it had been broken more than once, and he had one cauliflower ear. I didn't hesitate; I went right for the nose. I guess my punch broke it because he cried out as blood spurted everywhere. While I had the advantage, I reached inside his jacket and pulled out his weapon, which turned out to be a Glock. I proceeded to aim it at the Terrorist.

"All right, so we'll talk here," he said. "Tough guy, huh? Put that thing away. You know you're not going to shoot me."

"You never know."

He didn't seem the slightest bit concerned. In fact, he started to light up a cigar.

"I'm holding on to the weapon for leverage," I said. "I don't want anyone shooting me. Likewise, I'm not eager to do any harm. Now you want to talk? Let's do it here and now."

"I don't want you going around telling people, cops in particular, that I had a reason to whack the Priest."

"Except you did have reason, didn't you? Hadn't he agreed to help the Feds take you down?"

"I bore him no ill will. You think I don't know what's going on? I have my sources of information. He couldn't do me any harm. I knew what they were up to."

"I'm sure you did. But my clients aren't guilty of murder. All I'm doing is protecting their interests. I'm trying to find out who else might have had it in for Connolly. Nothing personal. It's just business."

"Now where have I heard that before?" Tony the Terrorist gave me a thin-lipped smile.

"I'll be looking at other leads."

"You do that. I might even throw some business your way," he said.

I was about to tell him not to bother, but didn't feel like pushing my luck.

"Get in," he said, gesturing irritably to his two goons. "And you, don't bleed all over the upholstery. Geez, this guy's worse than the Bayonne Bleeder."

The two hoods gave me lethal looks as they leveraged themselves back into the big car. I wasn't going to win any friends with that crowd. I decided to keep the automatic handy and apply for a gun permit as soon as possible.

✗   ✗   ✗   ✗

I told Lara about my little adventure later that afternoon.

She rubbed her arms as if she were feeling chilled. "I'm frightened for you," she said.

"Don't be. I can take care of myself."

She shook her head. "American gangsters, these are bad people. Very scary."

I didn't disagree with her. Obviously, the Terrorist had ears listening in high and low places. He was no one to mess with. I decided it was time to talk with Connolly's niece and nephew. I looked up their addresses and phone numbers and proceeded to make my first call.

Fiona Mallory answered her phone on the third ring. I explained who I was.

"I don't see why you're bothering me," she said in a hostile manner.

"Well, since you are one of your uncle's heirs, I have to assume you were close to him."

"Nobody was really close to Uncle Kevin. He wasn't that kind of person."

"Could we talk in person? I'll bring my legal assistant with me. She'll smack me around if I act rude."

That seemed to soften her attitude and she agreed to see me the following afternoon.

✗   ✗   ✗   ✗

Since Lara accompanied me, the drive proved pleasant. I got lost twice and it didn't even bother me.

Fiona Mallory's house was a modest dwelling in a blue-collar development not too different from the one in which my parents lived.

Fiona answered the door, with a small child of about two in her arms. The little girl clung to her mother, sucking her thumb.

"She's shy," Fiona said.

"What a beautiful child." Lara smiled and both the mother and child relaxed noticeably.

"Come in," Fiona said, leading us through to a shabby living room where toys were scattered. "Now what is it that you want to know about my uncle?"

"Did he have any enemies that you were aware of?"

We took seats on the sofa she indicated as she seated herself on a rocking chair. Fiona considered my question.

"He was very much respected and admired. It's only since the political climate changed and he became so ill that things changed."

I studied Fiona. She had dark red hair, blue eyes and a freckled face. She'd once been very pretty, but now she seemed tired, faded. I didn't want to offend her, but I had to ask some hard questions.

"I heard you say something to Dick Norris at your uncle's funeral about your uncle not leaving much money. I was told by a reliable source that he was very well off."

"I wish that were true. His house was heavily mortgaged. There wasn't much in savings. My brother and I could really use the money."

"Why is that?"

Lara got down and held her hand out to the little girl who finally left the protection of her mother's arms and approached Lara with interest.

"My husband and I split up last year. He had a girlfriend. He's a deadbeat dad. I have three children. My uncle used to help me out."

"And your brother?"

Fiona lowered her eyes. "You'll have to ask him yourself." She made it clear that our interview was over. I was frankly puzzled by what she'd said. Was she lying about the inheritance? If so, why?

As we left, I considered what to do next. As we got into the car, I pulled out my cell phone and dialed the number for Gerald O'Brien. He answered but was more suspicious and unfriendly than his sister.

"I can't think of any reason why I should talk to you."

"Well, as your uncle's heir, you might be considered a suspect in his death."

"Go to hell," he said and hung up.

"That went well," I said with an edge of sarcasm.

Lara eyed me sympathetically. "Perhaps he is hiding something."

"What if Gerald went to Connolly, asked for money and was refused? Could be a motive for murder." But I knew I was just offering supposition, painting a scenario without any form of evidence.

✗   ✗   ✗   ✗

"You have bugs in your office?" Dr. Jarvis asked. He was a potential client, a psychiatrist who appeared to be paranoid, another one of the people whose newspaper ad Mom responded to on my behalf.

"The place was fumigated last month," I said.

"I wasn't talking about insects," he said, shaking his head. "I'll just check for you. A person can never be too careful. All kinds of clever devices these days. I keep up on the technology. I have to. I've done work I can't tell you about. I've got to make certain no one's listening in on my conversations."

I let out a deep sigh. I didn't have to be a psychiatrist to know Jarvis was off. "Go right ahead and look around all you like," I told him.

He checked both desks, got down on his knees and looked everywhere. Then he examined my office phone. When he showed me the small listening device, I nearly fell off my chair.

Jarvis smiled at me and nodded with an I-told-you-so look. "Just as I thought."

But it wasn't Jarvis's office that had been bugged, it was mine. Someone wanted to hear what was going on. Why? All I had was a two-bit practice. Who could have the slightest interest in my conversations?

After Dr. Jarvis left my office, it suddenly hit me. It had to be related to Kevin Connolly. Who wire-tapped? The FBI? I could talk to Bill about it, but I doubted that Karen could or would fill me in. Then it occurred to me that Dr. Sarder and his partner might know something. As I considered our past discussions, I realized they hadn't shared everything they knew.

There was really only one way to straighten this mess out and it wasn't going to be in a courtroom. I wasn't exactly Perry Mason anyway. I had to get the people involved together. And just how was I going to manage that? I wasn't a magician either.

I started with a series of phone calls. First person I phoned was Dick Norris. As usual, his legal assistant gave me the runaround.

"Just tell your boss that if he doesn't call me back, Kevin Connolly's niece and nephew will be talking to the police and the FBI." I figured that would get his attention.

I decided to phone Bill. But I wanted privacy and so I left the office and took my cell phone into the men's bathroom. After making certain no one else was around, except for a pigeon roosting on the sill of an open window, I put in my call.

"My office is bugged," I told Bill as soon as he picked up. "Can Karen find out why the Feds would be interested in me?"

"I doubt it. No, my friend, you're on your own this time."

"Thanks a heap."

"Yeah, don't mention it. Give my regards to Lara; she's hot."

The phone was ringing as I re-entered my office.

"What are you after?" It was Dick Norris, sounding none too pleased.

"Same thing you are, protecting my clients' rights."

"Why the empty threat against Ms. Mallory and Mr. O'Brien?"

"I wasn't making any threats. I merely stated facts."

"What do you want?"

I gave myself a moment to think. "I want to set up a meeting in my office between my clients and yours."

"For what purpose?"

"Just to straighten out some matters related to Kevin Connolly's death. If they're not willing, they might have to talk to the police or the FBI instead."

"I don't like your attitude. You and your lowlife clients can come to my office."

I thought about what Lara had said. I would appear less like a professional if I went back to Norris's war room. It was important that I have an edge.

"This time it has to be my office. It's non-negotiable."

"All right. I'll talk to my clients and we'll get back to you about time."

I breathed a sigh of relief. He'd actually caved. "Make it tomorrow."

"I have court. I'll let you know." He slammed the receiver.

It was actually two days before I heard from Norris. Our conversation was short but not sweet. We set a meeting for the following afternoon. He sounded less than eager. Then I got busy making the rest of my calls.

⚔   ⚔   ⚔   ⚔

Lara had the coffee perking. I thought I knew how an actor must feel before a performance. I was sick to my stomach. I thought of my old man sneering at me like I was a screw-up. Well, maybe I hadn't been serious enough in school. But practicing law was a different matter entirely. I was paying attention, careful attention. This was serious business and I didn't intend to make any mistakes.

Dr. Sarder and Kala were the first to arrive. I was surprised that Mr. Banard was with them and said so.

"Mr. Banard is our both our friend and associate. We asked him to join us today." Dr. Sarder, Kala, and Banard took the more comfortable chairs that had come with the office. The extra chairs I'd borrowed from the test preparation firm down the hall were not nearly as good, but would have to do for the rest of the group.

Fiona Mallory, her brother Gerald O'Brien, and Dick Norris also arrived as a group. Norris herded his clients as far away as possible from my clients, which was not very far, considering the size of my office. The next to arrive was Lieutenant Monroe. I had invited one more individual but couldn't be certain he would show up.

They all looked at me expectantly. I cleared my throat and wiped my sweaty palms against my suit jacket.

"I've asked you here today to see if we can clear up the mystery of Kevin Connolly's murder, since we're all interested parties. Let me formally introduce my legal assistant, Lara Lopez. She previously worked as a prison psychologist. She knows a great deal about the workings of the criminal mind." They all turned to Lara and looked at her appraisingly.

"Good afternoon," she said, politely inclining her head, then sitting down at the second desk that was opposite mine, pen and legal pad at the ready.

"I discovered that my office was bugged," I said, deciding to be as blunt and forthright as possible.

Dr. Sarder jerked in his chair. Kala placed her hand on his and they exchanged a look.

"So I guess you knew about that?" I said turning to the doctor.

Dr. Sarder turned to Mr. Banard.

"I'm certain Dr. Sarder knows nothing about wire-tapping offices," Banard said, acting as a kind of informal spokesman.

"And I'm fairly certain that he does." I turned to Lieutenant Monroe. "Why would the Feds do that?"

Monroe shrugged. "Your clients are far from innocent people. Connolly had dirt on a lot of people, information he could trade. That included those two." He pointed accusingly at Dr. Sarder and Kala. "Don't know what the point of this is, Atkins. Seems to me you're just digging a deeper grave for your clients."

Suddenly, there was a commotion and the door to my office flew open. In marched Tony the Terminator Alfonso followed by a huge man who had to be six foot seven inches tall. The bodyguard looked like he'd wrestled professionally, or maybe had been a line-backer.

"Christ, this is your office? Can anybody be that poor?" He snapped his finger and the giant pulled a chair out for him. "I've seen bigger elevators." The bodyguard folded ham fists over his chest and stood behind Tony. "So what have I missed?"

"We were just discussing why my office was bugged."

"That hardly concerns my clients," Dick Norris said. "I resent you wasting our time."

"I have a question specifically for you," I shot back. "I have it from a reliable source that Kevin Connolly had a lot of money stashed away in unnumbered Swiss bank accounts."

"Just rumor, not fact," Norris said.

"Really? Because I thought it might be part of his estate. Yet Ms. Mallory told me there was actually very little left to her or her brother."

Norris pulled at his elegant shirt collar as if it were too tight. "As I said, I don't know where you got your information, but it doesn't happen to be true."

"I wish it were," Gerald O'Brien said. He and Tony the Termi-nator exchanged sharp looks.

"I know your uncle had plenty of cash," said Tony. "Everyone who wanted anything done in this state came to him. What kind of garbage are you pulling?" Tony's eyes narrowed as he stared at O'Brien, who looked ready to go into coronary arrest.

"You owe money to Mr. Alphonso?" I deduced.

Gerald O'Brien's gaze wouldn't meet my eyes.

"He owes me plenty," Tony said. "Claimed I'd be paid by his uncle."

"Why did O'Brien owe you money?" I asked.

"Gambling debts."

It was a sure thing that Kevin Connolly would not have wanted to pay off his nephew's gambling debts, not from what I knew about his personal values. Could O'Brien have decided to murder his uncle for a much-needed inheritance? That was a possibility. On the other hand, could Tony Alfonso have arranged that for Gerald?

"So did you provide a hit man for Gerald? The murder had a professional look to it. Don't you think so, Lieutenant?"

Tony jumped up from his chair. "Hey, I didn't provide any hit man to whack the Priest. I'm not in that kind of business."

"Yeah, right," Monroe said. "Why don't you tell us how you got the title *Terminator* fixed to your name."

"It seems to me you had every reason for wanting Kevin Connolly dead," I continued. "He was going to rat you out to the Feds, make your dealings public. Weren't they going to arrest you?"

Tony snorted. "Look, I was on to him. No way he was able to set me up. Talk to O'Brien. He was the one with a problem."

"My brother would never hurt Uncle Kevin," Fiona Mallory said, giving Tony a look that could fry ice. "And neither would I."

"This is a waste of our time," Norris said, rising to his feet. "My clients and I are ready to leave. Atkins, why don't you ask your client why he was willing to give up his lawsuit. You might learn something of interest."

Lieutenant Monroe moved toward Norris. "Why don't you stay a while? You obviously know a lot about this business, being Connolly's lawyer."

"Dr. Sarder, why did you decide to drop the lawsuit?" I asked. Norris had brought up a puzzling matter.

"It has nothing whatever to do with Mr. Connolly's death," he protested.

"It most certainly does," Norris countered.

I stared at my client. He in turn looked over at Kala, who nodded her head.

"It is all right," she said. "It no longer matters."

"Mr. Norris said that if we continued, Mr. Connolly would see to it that everyone knew that Kala and I were more than mere business partners."

"And is that true?" I probed.

"Yes, it's true," Kala answered when words seemed to fail Sarder. "You see, we both have families. Arthur has a wife and children. He does not live with them. He lives with me. But he doesn't wish to bring shame to his family. My husband and I are separated and have been for a number of years. My children are grown. Still, I would not like them embarrassed either. Kevin Connolly was a snake. Arthur and I hated him but we would not kill anyone."

"How did you meet Connolly in the first place?" I asked.

They both turned to Banard, who glanced up in alarm.

"So you're the one who told them that Connolly was the man to pay off if they wanted political clout?"

"I may have suggested something of the sort." Banard was just as oily as ever.

"I guess you collected money at both ends for the introduction."

"I thought you were my friend." Sarder turned an accusing look on Banard, who raised his hands as if warding off a physical attack.

"I assure you, I was told that Mr. Connolly was the most influential man in the state."

"And people call me a crook," Tony said with an amused grin. "Ha, bunch of hypocrites and liars."

"As I said before, there's no point in either myself or my clients remaining here," Dick Norris said, starting to rise again.

"We still haven't cleared up the matter of what happened to Connolly's stash of money," I said. "I've learned that if you want to solve certain crimes the way to do it is to follow the money. So let's see if there's a trail."

Norris shrugged. "If there were any accounts, they seem to have vanished."

"Somehow I doubt that. As Mr. Banard told Dr. Sarder, Kevin Connolly was a very powerful man. He was accustomed to taking bribes and payoffs. That was money he wouldn't want to account for to the IRS. So foreign accounts make a lot of sense. But he would have wanted at least his niece to have that money on his death. So Mr. Norris, as Connolly's attorney, he would have trusted you with that information."

Norris was on his feet and moving to toward the door. "Supposition, Atkins. I'm leaving."

Fiona Mallory, fiery redhead that she was, blocked his path looking incensed. "You said he left us very little. Did you take his money? Did you swindle him?"

"Dead men can't complain," I said. "Connolly could have turned you over to the Feds, Norris. Isn't that what he threatened to do? Is that why you killed him? Did he discover that you were embezzling money from his accounts?"

"I'm leaving," Norris said.

"Expect to hear from me," Lieutenant Monroe called to him. "We have some talking to do."

The door slammed.

"That crook!" Gerald O'Brien shouted.

"I think he murdered our uncle," Fiona stated, eyes flashing.

Tony Alphonso got to his feet and nodded to me. "You're a smart mouthpiece, kid. I'm definitely going to send you business." He snapped his fingers and the giant opened the door for him.

Dr. Sarder shook my hand. "You did as I asked, Mr. Atkins. You rolled the dice and won. Thank you."

It wasn't long before my office had emptied out. I turned to Lara. "So what are your dinner plans for tonight?"

"I was thinking of demonstrating my cooking skills for you," she said with a dimpled smile.

"A woman after my own heart. But I treat for groceries."

"A successful attorney like you, Mr. Atkins? I would expect nothing less."

We locked up the office and headed to the street below. Fresh air had never felt so good.

✗

Multiple award-winning author, Jacqueline (J.P.) Seewald, has taught creative, expository, and technical writing at Rutgers University as well as high school English. She also worked as both an academic librarian and an educational media specialist. Fifteen of her books of fiction have been published to critical praise including books for adults, teens, and children. Her short stories, poems, essays, reviews, and articles have appeared in hundreds of diverse publications and numerous anthologies such as: *The Writer*, *L.A. Times*, *Reader's Digest*, *Pedestal*, *Sherlock Holmes Mystery Magazine*, *Over My Dead Body!*, *Gumshoe Review*, *The Mystery Megapack*, *Library Journal*, and *Publishers Weekly*.

THE BOSCOMBE VALLEY MYSTERY

by Sir Arthur Conan Doyle

We were seated at breakfast one morning, my wife and I, when the maid brought in a telegram. It was from Sherlock Holmes and ran in this way:

"Have you a couple of days to spare? Have just been wired for from the west of England in connection with Boscombe Valley tragedy. Shall be glad if you will come with me. Air and scenery perfect. Leave Paddington by the 11:15."

"What do you say, dear?" said my wife, looking across at me. "Will you go?"

"I really don't know what to say. I have a fairly long list at present."

"Oh, Anstruther would do your work for you. You have been looking a little pale lately. I think that the change would do you good, and you are always so interested in Mr Sherlock Holmes's cases."

"I should be ungrateful if I were not, seeing what I gained through one of them," I answered. "But if I am to go, I must pack at once, for I have only half an hour."

My experience of camp life in Afghanistan had at least had the effect of making me a prompt and ready traveller. My wants were few and simple, so that in less than the time stated I was in a cab with my valise, rattling away to Paddington Station. Sherlock Holmes was pacing up and down the platform, his tall, gaunt figure made even gaunter and taller by his long grey travelling-cloak and close-fitting cloth cap.

"It is really very good of you to come, Watson," said he. "It makes a considerable difference to me, having someone with me on whom I can thoroughly rely. Local aid is always either worthless or else biased. If you will keep the two corner seats I shall get the tickets."

We had the carriage to ourselves save for an immense litter of papers which Holmes had brought with him. Among these he rummaged and read, with intervals of note-taking and of meditation, until we were past Reading. Then he suddenly rolled them all into a gigantic ball and tossed them up onto the rack.

"Have you heard anything of the case?" he asked.

"Not a word. I have not seen a paper for some days."

"The London press has not had very full accounts. I have just been looking through all the recent papers in order to master the particulars. It seems, from what I gather, to be one of those simple cases which are so extremely difficult."

"That sounds a little paradoxical."

"But it is profoundly true. Singularity is almost invariably a clue. The more featureless and commonplace a crime is, the more difficult it is to bring it home. In this case, however, they have established a very serious case against the son of the murdered man."

"It is a murder, then?"

"Well, it is conjectured to be so. I shall take nothing for granted until I have the opportunity of looking personally into it. I will explain the state of things to you, as far as I have been able to understand it, in a very few words.

"Boscombe Valley is a country district not very far from Ross, in Herefordshire. The largest landed proprietor in that part is a Mr John Turner, who made his money in Australia and returned some years ago to the old country. One of the farms which he held, that of Hatherley, was let to Mr Charles McCarthy, who was also an ex-Australian. The men had known each other in the colonies, so that it was not unnatural that when they came to settle down they should do so as near each other as possible. Turner was apparently the richer man, so McCarthy became his tenant but still remained, it seems, upon terms of perfect equality, as they were frequently together. McCarthy had one son, a lad of eighteen, and Turner had an only daughter of the same age, but neither of them had wives living. They appear to have avoided the society of the neighbouring English families and to have led retired lives, though both the McCarthys were fond of sport and were frequently seen at the race-meetings of the neighbourhood. McCarthy kept two servants—a man and a girl. Turner had a considerable household, some half-dozen at the least. That is as much as I have been able to gather about the families. Now for the facts.

"On June 3rd, that is, on Monday last, McCarthy left his house at Hatherley about three in the afternoon and walked down to the Boscombe Pool, which is a small lake formed by the spreading out of the stream which runs down the Boscombe Valley. He had been out with his serving-man in the morning at Ross, and he had told the man that he must hurry, as he had an appointment of importance to keep at three. From that appointment he never came back alive.

"From Hatherley Farm-house to the Boscombe Pool is a quarter of a mile, and two people saw him as he passed over this ground. One was an old woman, whose name is not mentioned, and the other was William Crowder, a game-keeper in the employ of Mr Turner. Both these witnesses depose that Mr McCarthy was walking alone. The game-keeper adds that within a few minutes of his seeing Mr McCarthy pass he had seen his son, Mr James McCarthy, going the same way with a gun under his arm. To the best of his belief, the father was actually in sight at the time, and the son was following him. He thought no more of the matter until he heard in the evening of the tragedy that had occurred.

"The two McCarthys were seen after the time when William Crowder, the game-keeper, lost sight of them. The Boscombe Pool is thickly wooded round, with just a fringe of grass and of reeds round the edge. A girl of fourteen, Patience Moran, who is the daughter of the lodge-keeper of the Boscombe Valley estate, was in one of the woods picking flowers. She states that while she was there she saw, at the border of the wood and close by the lake, Mr McCarthy and his son, and that they appeared to be having a violent quarrel. She heard Mr McCarthy the elder using very strong language to his son, and she saw the latter raise up his hand as if to strike his father. She was so frightened by their violence that she ran away and told her mother when she reached home that she had left the two McCarthys quarrelling near Boscombe Pool, and that she was afraid that they were going to fight. She had hardly said the words when young Mr McCarthy came running up to the lodge to say that he had found his father dead in the wood, and to ask for the help of the lodge-keeper. He was much excited, without either his gun or his hat, and his right hand and sleeve were observed to be stained with fresh blood. On following him they found the dead body stretched out upon the grass beside the pool. The head had been beaten in by repeated blows of some heavy and blunt weapon. The injuries were such as might very well have been inflicted by the butt-end of his son's gun, which was found lying on the grass within a few paces of the body. Under these circumstances the young man was instantly arrested, and a verdict of 'wilful murder' having been returned at the inquest on Tuesday, he was on Wednesday brought before the magistrates at Ross, who have referred the case to the next Assizes. Those are the main facts of the case as they came out before the coroner and the police-court."

"I could hardly imagine a more damning case," I remarked. "If ever circumstantial evidence pointed to a criminal it does so here."

"Circumstantial evidence is a very tricky thing," answered Holmes thoughtfully. "It may seem to point very straight to one thing, but if you shift your own point of view a little, you may find it pointing in an equally uncompromising manner to something entirely different. It must be confessed, however, that the case looks exceedingly grave against the young man, and it is very possible that he is indeed the culprit. There are several people in the neighbourhood, however, and among them Miss Turner, the daughter of the neighbouring landowner, who believe in his innocence, and who have retained Lestrade, whom you may recollect in connection with the Study in Scarlet, to work out the case in his interest. Lestrade, being rather puzzled, has referred the case to me, and hence it is that two middle-aged gentlemen are flying westward at fifty miles an hour instead of quietly digesting their breakfasts at home."

"I am afraid," said I, "that the facts are so obvious that you will find little credit to be gained out of this case."

"There is nothing more deceptive than an obvious fact," he answered, laughing. "Besides, we may chance to hit upon some other obvious facts which may have been by no means obvious to Mr Lestrade. You know me too well to think that I am boasting when I say that I shall either confirm or destroy his theory by means which he is quite incapable of employing, or even of understanding. To take the first example to hand, I very clearly perceive that in your bedroom the window is upon the right-hand side, and yet I question whether Mr Lestrade would have noted even so self-evident a thing as that."

"How on earth—"

"My dear fellow, I know you well. I know the military neatness which characterises you. You shave every morning, and in this season you shave by the sunlight; but since your shaving is less and less complete as we get farther back on the left side, until it becomes positively slovenly as we get round the angle of the jaw, it is surely very clear that that side is less illuminated than the other. I could not imagine a man of your habits looking at himself in an equal light and being satisfied with such a result. I only quote this as a trivial example of observation and inference. Therein lies my métier, and it is just possible that it may be of some service in the investigation which lies before us. There are one or two minor points which were brought out in the inquest, and which are worth considering."

"What are they?"

"It appears that his arrest did not take place at once, but after the return to Hatherley Farm. On the inspector of constabulary informing him that he was a prisoner, he remarked that he was not surprised to hear it, and that it was no more than his deserts. This observation of his had the natural effect of removing any traces of doubt which might have remained in the minds of the coroner's jury."

"It was a confession," I ejaculated.

"No, for it was followed by a protestation of innocence."

"Coming on the top of such a damning series of events, it was at least a most suspicious remark."

"On the contrary," said Holmes, "it is the brightest rift which I can at present see in the clouds. However innocent he might be, he could not be such an absolute imbecile as not to see that the circumstances were very black against him. Had he appeared surprised at his own arrest, or feigned indignation at it, I should have looked upon it as highly suspicious, because such surprise or anger would not be natural under the circumstances, and yet might appear to be the best policy to a scheming man. His frank acceptance of the situation marks him as either an innocent man, or else as a man of considerable self-restraint and firmness. As to his remark about his deserts, it was also not unnatural if you consider that he stood beside the dead body of his father, and that there is no doubt that he had that very day so far forgotten his filial duty as to bandy words with him, and even, according to the little girl whose evidence is so important, to raise his hand as if to strike him. The self-reproach and contrition which are displayed in his remark appear to me to be the signs of a healthy mind rather than of a guilty one."

I shook my head. "Many men have been hanged on far slighter evidence," I remarked.

"So they have. And many men have been wrongfully hanged."

"What is the young man's own account of the matter?"

"It is, I am afraid, not very encouraging to his supporters, though there are one or two points in it which are suggestive. You will find it here, and may read it for yourself."

He picked out from his bundle a copy of the local Hereford-shire paper, and having turned down the sheet he pointed out the paragraph in which the unfortunate young man had given his own statement of what had occurred. I settled myself down in the corner of the carriage and read it very carefully. It ran in this way:

"Mr James McCarthy, the only son of the deceased, was then called and gave evidence as follows: 'I had been away from home for three days at Bristol, and had only just returned upon the morning of last Monday, the 3rd. My father was absent from home at the time of my arrival, and I was informed by the maid that he had driven over to Ross with John Cobb, the groom. Shortly after my return I heard the wheels of his trap in the yard, and, looking out of my window, I saw him get out and walk rapidly out of the yard, though I was not aware in which direction he was going. I then took my gun and strolled out in the direction of the Boscombe Pool, with the intention of visiting the rabbit warren which is upon the other side. On my way I saw William Crowder, the game-keeper, as he had stated in his evidence; but he is mistaken in thinking that I was following my father. I had no idea that he was in front of me. When about a hundred yards from the pool I heard a cry of "Cooee!" which was a usual signal between my father and myself. I then hurried forward, and found him standing by the pool. He appeared to be much surprised at seeing me and asked me rather roughly what I was doing there. A conversation ensued which led to high words and almost to blows, for my father was a man of a very violent temper. Seeing that his passion was becoming ungovernable, I left him and returned towards Hatherley Farm. I had not gone more than 150 yards, however, when I heard a hideous outcry behind me, which caused me to run back again. I found my father expiring upon the ground, with his head terribly injured. I dropped my gun and held him in my arms, but he almost instantly expired. I knelt beside him for some minutes, and then made my way to Mr Turner's lodge-keeper, his house being the nearest, to ask for assistance. I saw no one near my father when I returned, and I have no idea how he came by his injuries. He was not a popular man, being somewhat cold and forbidding in his manners, but he had, as far as I know, no active enemies. I know nothing further of the matter.'

"The Coroner: Did your father make any statement to you before he died?

"Witness: He mumbled a few words, but I could only catch some allusion to a rat.

"The Coroner: What did you understand by that?

"Witness: It conveyed no meaning to me. I thought that he was delirious.

"The Coroner: What was the point upon which you and your father had this final quarrel?

"Witness: I should prefer not to answer.

"The Coroner: I am afraid that I must press it.

"Witness: It is really impossible for me to tell you. I can assure you that it has nothing to do with the sad tragedy which followed.

"The Coroner: That is for the court to decide. I need not point out to you that your refusal to answer will prejudice your case considerably in any future proceedings which may arise.

"Witness: I must still refuse.

"The Coroner: I understand that the cry of 'Cooee' was a common signal between you and your father?

"Witness: It was.

"The Coroner: How was it, then, that he uttered it before he saw you, and before he even knew that you had returned from Bristol?

"Witness (with considerable confusion): I do not know.

"A Juryman: Did you see nothing which aroused your suspicions when you returned on hearing the cry and found your father fatally injured?

"Witness: Nothing definite.

"The Coroner: What do you mean?

"Witness: I was so disturbed and excited as I rushed out into the open, that I could think of nothing except of my father. Yet I have a vague impression that as I ran forward something lay upon the ground to the left of me. It seemed to me to be something grey in colour, a coat of some sort, or a plaid, perhaps. When I rose from my father I looked round for it, but it was gone.

"'Do you mean that it disappeared before you went for help?'

"'Yes, it was gone.'

"'You cannot say what it was?'

"'No, I had a feeling something was there.'

"'How far from the body?'

"'A dozen yards or so.'

"'And how far from the edge of the wood?'

"'About the same.'

"'Then if it was removed it was while you were within a dozen yards of it?'

"'Yes, but with my back towards it.'

"This concluded the examination of the witness."

"I see," said I as I glanced down the column, "that the coroner in his concluding remarks was rather severe upon young McCarthy. He calls attention, and with reason, to the discrepancy about his father having signalled to him before seeing him, also to his refusal to give details of his conversation with his father, and his singular account of his father's dying words. They are all, as he remarks, very much against the son."

Holmes laughed softly to himself and stretched himself out upon the cushioned seat. "Both you and the coroner have been at some pains," said he, "to single out the very strongest points in the young man's favour. Don't you see that you alternately give him credit for having too much imagination and too little? Too little, if he could not invent a cause of quarrel which would give him the sympathy of the jury; too much, if he evolved from his own inner consciousness anything so outré as a dying reference to a rat, and the incident of the vanishing cloth. No, sir, I shall approach this case from the point of view that what this young man says is true, and we shall see whither that hypothesis will lead us. And now here is my pocket Petrarch, and not another word shall I say of this case until we are on the scene of action. We lunch at Swindon, and I see that we shall be there in twenty minutes."

It was nearly four o'clock when we at last, after passing through the beautiful Stroud Valley, and over the broad gleaming Severn, found ourselves at the pretty little country-town of Ross. A lean, ferret-like man, furtive and sly-looking, was waiting for us upon the platform. In spite of the light brown dustcoat and leather-leggings which he wore in deference to his rustic surroundings, I had no difficulty in recognising Lestrade, of Scotland Yard. With him we drove to the Hereford Arms where a room had already been engaged for us.

"I have ordered a carriage," said Lestrade as we sat over a cup of tea. "I knew your energetic nature, and that you would not be happy until you had been on the scene of the crime."

"It was very nice and complimentary of you," Holmes answered. "It is entirely a question of barometric pressure."

Lestrade looked startled. "I do not quite follow," he said.

"How is the glass? Twenty-nine, I see. No wind, and not a cloud in the sky. I have a caseful of cigarettes here which need smoking, and the sofa is very much superior to the usual country hotel abomination. I do not think that it is probable that I shall use the carriage to-night."

Lestrade laughed indulgently. "You have, no doubt, already formed your conclusions from the newspapers," he said. "The case is as plain as a pikestaff, and the more one goes into it the plainer it becomes. Still, of course, one can't refuse a lady, and such a very positive one, too. She has heard of you, and would have your opinion, though I repeatedly told her that there was nothing which you could do which I had not already done. Why, bless my soul! Here is her carriage at the door."

He had hardly spoken before there rushed into the room one of the most lovely young women that I have ever seen in my life. Her violet eyes shining, her lips parted, a pink flush upon her cheeks, all thought of her natural reserve lost in her overpowering excitement and concern.

"Oh, Mr Sherlock Holmes!" she cried, glancing from one to the other of us, and finally, with a woman's quick intuition, fastening upon my companion, "I am so glad that you have come. I have driven down to tell you so. I know that James didn't do it. I know it, and I want you to start upon your work knowing it, too. Never let yourself doubt upon that point. We have known each other since we were little children, and I know his faults as no one else does; but he is too tender-hearted to hurt a fly. Such a charge is absurd to anyone who really knows him."

"I hope we may clear him, Miss Turner," said Sherlock Holmes. "You may rely upon my doing all that I can."

"But you have read the evidence. You have formed some conclusion? Do you not see some loophole, some flaw? Do you not yourself think that he is innocent?"

"I think that it is very probable."

"There, now!" she cried, throwing back her head and looking defiantly at Lestrade. "You hear! He gives me hopes."

Lestrade shrugged his shoulders. "I am afraid that my colleague has been a little quick in forming his conclusions," he said.

"But he is right. Oh! I know that he is right. James never did it. And about his quarrel with his father, I am sure that the reason why he would not speak about it to the coroner was because I was concerned in it."

"In what way?" asked Holmes.

"It is no time for me to hide anything. James and his father had many disagreements about me. Mr McCarthy was very anxious that there should be a marriage between us. James and I have always loved each other as brother and sister; but of course he is young and has seen very little of life yet, and—and—well, he naturally did not wish to do anything like that yet. So there were quarrels, and this, I am sure, was one of them."

"And your father?" asked Holmes. "Was he in favour of such a union?"

"No, he was averse to it, also. No one but Mr McCarthy was in favour of it." A quick blush passed over her fresh young face as Holmes shot one of his keen, questioning glances at her.

"Thank you for this information," said he. "May I see your father if I call to-morrow?"

"I am afraid the doctor won't allow it."

"The doctor?"

"Yes, have you not heard? Poor father has never been strong for years back, but this has broken him down completely. He has taken to his bed, and Dr Willows says that he is a wreck and that his nervous system is shattered. Mr McCarthy was the only man alive who had known Dad in the old days in Victoria."

"Ha! In Victoria! That is important."

"Yes, at the mines."

"Quite so; at the gold-mines, where, as I understand, Mr Turner made his money."

"Yes, certainly."

"Thank you, Miss Turner. You have been of material assistance to me."

"You will tell me if you have any news to-morrow. No doubt you will go to the prison to see James. Oh, if you do, Mr Holmes, do tell him that I know him to be innocent."

"I will, Miss Turner."

"I must go home now, for dad is very ill, and he misses me so if I leave him. Good-bye, and God help you in your undertaking." She hurried from the room as impulsively as she had entered, and we heard the wheels of her carriage rattle off down the street.

"I am ashamed of you, Holmes," said Lestrade with dignity after a few minutes' silence. "Why should you raise up hopes which you are bound to disappoint? I am not over-tender of heart, but I call it cruel."

"I think that I see my way to clearing James McCarthy," said Holmes. "Have you an order to see him in prison?"

"Yes, but only for you and me."

"Then I shall reconsider my resolution about going out. We have still time to take a train to Hereford and see him to-night?"

"Ample."

"Then let us do so. Watson, I fear that you will find it very slow, but I shall only be away a couple of hours."

I walked down to the station with them, and then wandered through the streets of the little town, finally returning to the hotel, where I lay upon the sofa and tried to interest myself in a yellow-backed novel. The puny plot of the story was so thin, however, when compared to the deep mystery through which we were groping, and I found my attention wander so continually from the action to the fact, that I at last flung it across the room and gave myself up entirely to a consideration of the events of the day. Supposing that this unhappy young man's story were absolutely true, then what hellish thing, what absolutely unforeseen and extraordinary calamity could have occurred between the time when he parted from his father, and the moment when, drawn back by his screams, he rushed into the glade? It was something terrible and deadly. What could it be? Might not the nature of the injuries reveal something to my medical instincts? I rang the bell and called for the weekly county paper, which contained a verbatim account of the inquest. In the surgeon's deposition it was stated that the posterior third of the left parietal bone and the left half of the occipital bone had been shattered by a heavy blow from a blunt weapon. I marked the spot upon my own head. Clearly such a blow must have been struck from behind. That was to some extent in favour of the accused, as when seen quarrelling he was face to face with his father. Still, it did not go for very much, for the older man might have turned his back before the blow fell. Still, it might be worth while to call Holmes's attention to it. Then there was the peculiar dying reference to a rat. What could that mean? It could not be delirium. A man dying from a sudden blow does not commonly become delirious. No, it was more likely to be an attempt to explain how he met his fate. But what could it indicate? I cudgelled my brains to find some possible explanation. And then the incident of the grey cloth seen by young McCarthy. If that were true the murderer must have dropped some part of his dress, presumably his overcoat, in his flight, and must have had the hardihood to return and to carry it away at the instant when the son was kneeling with his back turned not a dozen paces off. What a tissue of mysteries and improbabilities the whole thing was! I did not wonder at Lestrade's opinion, and yet I had so much faith in Sherlock Holmes's insight that I could not lose hope as long as every fresh fact seemed to strengthen his conviction of young McCarthy's innocence.

It was late before Sherlock Holmes returned. He came back alone, for Lestrade was staying in lodgings in the town.

"The glass still keeps very high," he remarked as he sat down. "It is of importance that it should not rain before we are able to go over the ground. On the other hand, a man should be at his very best and keenest for such nice work as that, and I did not wish to do it when fagged by a long journey. I have seen young McCarthy."

"And what did you learn from him?"

"Nothing."

"Could he throw no light?"

"None at all. I was inclined to think at one time that he knew who had done it and was screening him or her, but I am convinced now that he is as puzzled as everyone else. He is not a very quick-witted youth, though comely to look at and, I should think, sound at heart."

"I cannot admire his taste," I remarked, "if it is indeed a fact that he was averse to a marriage with so charming a young lady as this Miss Turner."

"Ah, thereby hangs a rather painful tale. This fellow is madly, insanely, in love with her, but some two years ago, when he was only a lad, and before he really knew her, for she had been away five years at a boarding-school, what does the idiot do but get into the clutches of a barmaid in Bristol and marry her at a registry office? No one knows a word of the matter, but you can imagine how maddening it must be to him to be upbraided for not doing what he would give his very eyes to do, but what he knows to be absolutely impossible. It was sheer frenzy of this sort which made him throw his hands up into the air when his father, at their last interview, was goading him on to propose to Miss Turner. On the other hand, he had no means of supporting himself, and his father, who was by all accounts a very hard man, would have thrown him over utterly had he known the truth. It was with his barmaid wife that he had spent the last three days in Bristol, and his father did not know where he was. Mark that point. It is of importance. Good has come out of evil, however, for the barmaid, finding from the papers that he is in serious trouble and likely to be hanged, has thrown him over utterly and has written to him to say that she has a husband already in the Bermuda Dockyard, so that there is really no tie between them. I think that that bit of news has consoled young McCarthy for all that he has suffered."

"But if he is innocent, who has done it?"

"Ah! Who? I would call your attention very particularly to two points. One is that the murdered man had an appointment with someone at the pool, and that the someone could not have been his son, for his son was away, and he did not know when he would return. The second is that the murdered man was heard to cry 'Cooee!' before he knew that his son had returned. Those are the crucial points upon which the case depends. And now let us talk about George Meredith, if you please, and we shall leave all minor matters until to-morrow."

✗   ✗   ✗   ✗

There was no rain, as Holmes had foretold, and the morning broke bright and cloudless. At nine o'clock Lestrade called for us with the carriage, and we set off for Hatherley Farm and the Boscombe Pool.

"There is serious news this morning," Lestrade observed. "It is said that Mr Turner, of the Hall, is so ill that his life is despaired of."

"An elderly man, I presume?" said Holmes.

"About sixty; but his constitution has been shattered by his life abroad, and he has been in failing health for some time. This business has had a very bad effect upon him. He was an old friend of McCarthy's, and, I may add, a great benefactor to him, for I have learned that he gave him Hatherley Farm rent free."

"Indeed! That is interesting," said Holmes.

"Oh, yes! In a hundred other ways he has helped him. Everybody about here speaks of his kindness to him."

"Really! Does it not strike you as a little singular that this McCarthy, who appears to have had little of his own, and to have been under such obligations to Turner, should still talk of marrying his son to Turner's daughter, who is, presumably, heiress to the estate, and that in such a very cocksure manner, as if it were merely a case of a proposal and all else would follow? It is the more strange, since we know that Turner himself was averse to the idea. The daughter told us as much. Do you not deduce something from that?"

"We have got to the deductions and the inferences," said Lestrade, winking at me. "I find it hard enough to tackle facts, Holmes, without flying away after theories and fancies."

"You are right," said Holmes demurely; "you do find it very hard to tackle the facts."

"Anyhow, I have grasped one fact which you seem to find it difficult to get hold of," replied Lestrade with some warmth.

"And that is—"

"That McCarthy senior met his death from McCarthy junior and that all theories to the contrary are the merest moonshine."

"Well, moonshine is a brighter thing than fog," said Holmes, laughing. "But I am very much mistaken if this is not Hatherley Farm upon the left."

"Yes, that is it." It was a widespread, comfortable-looking building, two-storied, slate-roofed, with great yellow blotches of lichen upon the grey walls. The drawn blinds and the smokeless chimneys, however, gave it a stricken look, as though the weight of this horror still lay heavy upon it. We called at the door, when the maid, at Holmes's request, showed us the boots which her master wore at the time of his death, and also a pair of the son's, though not the pair which he had then had. Having measured these very carefully from seven or eight different points, Holmes desired to be led to the court-yard, from which we all followed the winding track which led to Boscombe Pool.

Sherlock Holmes was transformed when he was hot upon such a scent as this. Men who had only known the quiet thinker and logician of Baker Street would have failed to recognise him. His face flushed and darkened. His brows were drawn into two hard black lines, while his eyes shone out from beneath them with a steely glitter. His face was bent downward, his shoulders bowed, his lips compressed, and the veins stood out like whipcord in his long, sinewy neck. His nostrils seemed to dilate with a purely animal lust for the chase, and his mind was so absolutely concentrated upon the matter before him that a question or remark fell unheeded upon his ears, or, at the most, only provoked a quick, impatient snarl in reply. Swiftly and silently he made his way along the track which ran through the meadows, and so by way of the woods to the Boscombe Pool. It was damp, marshy ground, as is all that district, and there were marks of many feet, both upon the path and amid the short grass which bounded it on either side. Sometimes Holmes would hurry on, sometimes stop dead, and once he made quite a little detour into the meadow. Lestrade and I walked behind him, the detective indifferent and contemptuous, while I watched my friend with the interest which sprang from the conviction that every one of his actions was directed towards a definite end.

The Boscombe Pool, which is a little reed-girt sheet of water some fifty yards across, is situated at the boundary between the Hatherley Farm and the private park of the wealthy Mr Turner. Above the woods which lined it upon the farther side we could see the red, jutting pinnacles which marked the site of the rich landowner's dwelling. On the Hatherley side of the pool the woods grew very thick, and there was a narrow belt of sodden grass twenty paces across between the edge of the trees and the reeds which lined the lake. Lestrade showed us the exact spot at which the body had been found, and, indeed, so moist was the ground, that I could plainly see the traces which had been left by the fall of the stricken man. To Holmes, as I could see by his eager face and peering eyes, very many other things were to be read upon the trampled grass. He ran round, like a dog who is picking up a scent, and then turned upon my companion.

"What did you go into the pool for?" he asked.

"I fished about with a rake. I thought there might be some weapon or other trace. But how on earth—"

"Oh, tut, tut! I have no time! That left foot of yours with its inward twist is all over the place. A mole could trace it, and there it vanishes among the reeds. Oh, how simple it would all have been had I been here before they came like a herd of buffalo and wallowed all over it. Here is where the party with the lodge-keeper came, and they have covered all tracks for six or eight feet round the body. But here are three separate tracks of the same feet." He drew out a lens and lay down upon his waterproof to have a better view, talking all the time rather to himself than to us. "These are young McCarthy's feet. Twice he was walking, and once he ran swiftly, so that the soles are deeply marked and the heels hardly visible. That bears out his story. He ran when he saw his father on the ground. Then here are the father's feet as he paced up and down. What is this, then? It is the butt-end of the gun as the son stood listening. And this? Ha, ha! What have we here? Tiptoes! Tiptoes! Square, too, quite unusual boots! They come, they go, they come again—of course that was for the cloak. Now where did they come from?" He ran up and down, sometimes losing, sometimes finding the track until we were well within the edge of the wood and under the shadow of a great beech, the largest tree in the neighbourhood. Holmes traced his way to the farther side of this and lay down once more upon his face with a little cry of satisfaction. For a long time he remained there, turning over the leaves and dried sticks, gathering up what seemed to me to be dust into an envelope and examining with his lens not only the ground but even the bark of the tree as far as he could reach. A jagged stone was lying among the moss, and this also he carefully examined and retained. Then he followed a pathway through the wood until he came to the highroad, where all traces were lost.

"It has been a case of considerable interest," he remarked, returning to his natural manner. "I fancy that this grey house on the right must be the lodge. I think that I will go in and have a word with Moran, and perhaps write a little note. Having done that, we may drive back to our luncheon. You may walk to the cab, and I shall be with you presently."

It was about ten minutes before we regained our cab and drove back into Ross, Holmes still carrying with him the stone which he had picked up in the wood.

"This may interest you, Lestrade," he remarked, holding it out. "The murder was done with it."

"I see no marks."

"There are none."

"How do you know, then?"

"The grass was growing under it. It had only lain there a few days. There was no sign of a place whence it had been taken. It corresponds with the injuries. There is no sign of any other weapon."

"And the murderer?"

"Is a tall man, left-handed, limps with the right leg, wears thick-soled shooting-boots and a grey cloak, smokes Indian cigars, uses a cigar-holder, and carries a blunt pen-knife in his pocket. There are several other indications, but these may be enough to aid us in our search."

Lestrade laughed. "I am afraid that I am still a sceptic," he said. "Theories are all very well, but we have to deal with a hard-headed British jury."

"*Nous verrons*," answered Holmes calmly. "You work your own method, and I shall work mine. I shall be busy this afternoon, and shall probably return to London by the evening train."

"And leave your case unfinished?"

"No, finished."

"But the mystery?"

"It is solved."

"Who was the criminal, then?"

"The gentleman I describe."

"But who is he?"

"Surely it would not be difficult to find out. This is not such a populous neighbourhood."

Lestrade shrugged his shoulders. "I am a practical man," he said, "and I really cannot undertake to go about the country looking for a left-handed gentleman with a game leg. I should become the laughing-stock of Scotland Yard."

"All right," said Holmes quietly. "I have given you the chance. Here are your lodgings. Good-bye. I shall drop you a line before I leave."

Having left Lestrade at his rooms, we drove to our hotel, where we found lunch upon the table. Holmes was silent and buried in thought with a pained expression upon his face, as one who finds himself in a perplexing position.

"Look here, Watson," he said when the cloth was cleared, "just sit down in this chair and let me preach to you for a little. I don't know quite what to do, and I should value your advice. Light a cigar and let me expound."

"Pray do so."

"Well, now, in considering this case there are two points about young McCarthy's narrative which struck us both instantly, although they impressed me in his favour and you against him. One was the fact that his father should, according to his account, cry 'Cooee!' before seeing him. The other was his singular dying reference to a rat. He mumbled several words, you understand, but that was all that caught the son's ear. Now from this double point our research must commence, and we will begin it by presuming that what the lad says is absolutely true."

"What of this 'Cooee!' then?"

"Well, obviously it could not have been meant for the son. The son, as far as he knew, was in Bristol. It was mere chance that he was within earshot. The 'Cooee!' was meant to attract the attention of whoever it was that he had the appointment with. But 'Cooee' is a distinctly Australian cry, and one which is used between Australians. There is a strong presumption that the person whom McCarthy expected to meet him at Boscombe Pool was someone who had been in Australia."

"What of the rat, then?"

Sherlock Holmes took a folded paper from his pocket and flattened it out on the table. "This is a map of the Colony of Victoria," he said. "I wired to Bristol for it last night." He put his hand over part of the map. "What do you read?"

"ARAT," I read.

"And now?" He raised his hand.

"BALLARAT."

"Quite so. That was the word the man uttered, and of which his son only caught the last two syllables. He was trying to utter the name of his murderer. So and so, of Ballarat."

"It is wonderful!" I exclaimed.

"It is obvious. And now, you see, I had narrowed the field down considerably. The possession of a grey garment was a third point which, granting the son's statement to be correct, was a certainty. We have come now out of mere vagueness to the definite conception of an Australian from Ballarat with a grey cloak."

"Certainly."

"And one who was at home in the district, for the pool can only be approached by the farm or by the estate, where strangers could hardly wander."

"Quite so."

"Then comes our expedition of to-day. By an examination of the ground I gained the trifling details which I gave to that imbecile Lestrade, as to the personality of the criminal."

"But how did you gain them?"

"You know my method. It is founded upon the observation of trifles."

"His height I know that you might roughly judge from the length of his stride. His boots, too, might be told from their traces."

"Yes, they were peculiar boots."

"But his lameness?"

"The impression of his right foot was always less distinct than his left. He put less weight upon it. Why? Because he limped—he was lame."

"But his left-handedness."

"You were yourself struck by the nature of the injury as recorded by the surgeon at the inquest. The blow was struck from immediately behind, and yet was upon the left side. Now, how can that be unless it were by a left-handed man? He had stood behind that tree during the interview between the father and son. He had even smoked there. I found the ash of a cigar, which my special knowledge of tobacco ashes enables me to pronounce as an Indian cigar. I have, as you know, devoted some attention to this, and written a little monograph on the ashes of 140 different varieties of pipe, cigar, and cigarette tobacco. Having found the ash, I then looked round and discovered the stump among the moss where he had tossed it. It was an Indian cigar, of the variety which are rolled in Rotterdam."

"And the cigar-holder?"

"I could see that the end had not been in his mouth. Therefore he used a holder. The tip had been cut off, not bitten off, but the cut was not a clean one, so I deduced a blunt pen-knife."

"Holmes," I said, "you have drawn a net round this man from which he cannot escape, and you have saved an innocent human life as truly as if you had cut the cord which was hanging him. I see the direction in which all this points. The culprit is—"

"Mr John Turner," cried the hotel waiter, opening the door of our sitting-room, and ushering in a visitor.

The man who entered was a strange and impressive figure. His slow, limping step and bowed shoulders gave the appearance of decrepitude, and yet his hard, deep-lined, craggy features, and his enormous limbs showed that he was possessed of unusual strength of body and of character. His tangled beard, grizzled hair, and outstanding, drooping eyebrows combined to give an air of dignity and power to his appearance, but his face was of an ashen white, while his lips and the corners of his nostrils were tinged with a shade of blue. It was clear to me at a glance that he was in the grip of some deadly and chronic disease.

"Pray sit down on the sofa," said Holmes gently. "You had my note?"

"Yes, the lodge-keeper brought it up. You said that you wished to see me here to avoid scandal."

"I thought people would talk if I went to the Hall."

"And why did you wish to see me?" He looked across at my companion with despair in his weary eyes, as though his question was already answered.

"Yes," said Holmes, answering the look rather than the words. "It is so. I know all about McCarthy."

The old man sank his face in his hands. "God help me!" he cried. "But I would not have let the young man come to harm. I give you my word that I would have spoken out if it went against him at the Assizes."

"I am glad to hear you say so," said Holmes gravely.

"I would have spoken now had it not been for my dear girl. It would break her heart—it will break her heart when she hears that I am arrested."

"It may not come to that," said Holmes.

"What?"

"I am no official agent. I understand that it was your daughter who required my presence here, and I am acting in her interests. Young McCarthy must be got off, however."

"I am a dying man," said old Turner. "I have had diabetes for years. My doctor says it is a question whether I shall live a month. Yet I would rather die under my own roof than in a gaol."

Holmes rose and sat down at the table with his pen in his hand and a bundle of paper before him. "Just tell us the truth," he said. "I shall jot down the facts. You will sign it, and Watson here can witness it. Then I could produce your confession at the last extremity to save young McCarthy. I promise you that I shall not use it unless it is absolutely needed."

"It's as well," said the old man; "it's a question whether I shall live to the Assizes, so it matters little to me, but I should wish to spare Alice the shock. And now I will make the thing clear to you; it has been a long time in the acting, but will not take me long to tell.

"You didn't know this dead man, McCarthy. He was a devil incarnate. I tell you that. God keep you out of the clutches of such a man as he. His grip has been upon me these twenty years, and he has blasted my life. I'll tell you first how I came to be in his power.

"It was in the early '60's at the diggings. I was a young chap then, hot-blooded and reckless, ready to turn my hand at anything; I got among bad companions, took to drink, had no luck with my claim, took to the bush, and in a word became what you would call over here a highway robber. There were six of us, and we had a wild, free life of it, sticking up a station from time to time, or stopping the wagons on the road to the diggings. Black Jack of Ballarat was the name I went under, and our party is still remembered in the colony as the Ballarat Gang.

"One day a gold convoy came down from Ballarat to Melbourne, and we lay in wait for it and attacked it. There were six troopers and six of us, so it was a close thing, but we emptied four of their saddles at the first volley. Three of our boys were killed, however, before we got the swag. I put my pistol to the head of the wagon-driver, who was this very man McCarthy. I wish to the Lord that I had shot him then, but I spared him, though I saw his wicked little eyes fixed on my face, as though to remember every feature. We got away with the gold, became wealthy men, and made our way over to England without being suspected. There I parted from my old pals and determined to settle down to a quiet and respectable life. I bought this estate, which chanced to be in the market, and I set myself to do a little good with my money, to make up for the way in which I had earned it. I married, too, and though my wife died young she left me my dear little Alice. Even when she was just a baby her wee hand seemed to lead me down the right path as nothing else had ever done. In a word, I turned over a new leaf and did my best to make up for the past. All was going well when McCarthy laid his grip upon me.

"I had gone up to town about an investment, and I met him in Regent Street with hardly a coat to his back or a boot to his foot.

"'Here we are, Jack,' says he, touching me on the arm; 'we'll be as good as a family to you. There's two of us, me and my son, and you can have the keeping of us. If you don't—it's a fine, law-abiding country is England, and there's always a policeman within hail.'

"Well, down they came to the west country, there was no shaking them off, and there they have lived rent free on my best land ever since. There was no rest for me, no peace, no forgetfulness; turn where I would, there was his cunning, grinning face at my elbow. It grew worse as Alice grew up, for he soon saw I was more afraid of her knowing my past than of the police. Whatever he wanted he must have, and whatever it was I gave him without question, land, money, houses, until at last he asked a thing which I could not give. He asked for Alice.

"His son, you see, had grown up, and so had my girl, and as I was known to be in weak health, it seemed a fine stroke to him that his lad should step into the whole property. But there I was firm. I would not have his cursed stock mixed with mine; not that

I had any dislike to the lad, but his blood was in him, and that was enough. I stood firm. McCarthy threatened. I braved him to do his worst. We were to meet at the pool midway between our houses to talk it over.

"When I went down there I found him talking with his son, so I smoked a cigar and waited behind a tree until he should be alone. But as I listened to his talk all that was black and bitter in me seemed to come uppermost. He was urging his son to marry my daughter with as little regard for what she might think as if she were a slut from off the streets. It drove me mad to think that I and all that I held most dear should be in the power of such a man as this. Could I not snap the bond? I was already a dying and a desperate man. Though clear of mind and fairly strong of limb, I knew that my own fate was sealed. But my memory and my girl! Both could be saved if I could but silence that foul tongue. I did it, Mr Holmes. I would do it again. Deeply as I have sinned, I have led a life of martyrdom to atone for it. But that my girl should be entangled in the same meshes which held me was more than I could suffer. I struck him down with no more compunction than if he had been some foul and venomous beast. His cry brought back his son; but I had gained the cover of the wood, though I was forced to go back to fetch the cloak which I had dropped in my flight. That is the true story, gentlemen, of all that occurred."

"Well, it is not for me to judge you," said Holmes as the old man signed the statement which had been drawn out. "I pray that we may never be exposed to such a temptation."

"I pray not, sir. And what do you intend to do?"

"In view of your health, nothing. You are yourself aware that you will soon have to answer for your deed at a higher court than the Assizes. I will keep your confession, and if McCarthy is condemned I shall be forced to use it. If not, it shall never be seen by mortal eye; and your secret, whether you be alive or dead, shall be safe with us."

"Farewell, then," said the old man solemnly. "Your own death-beds, when they come, will be the easier for the thought of the peace which you have given to mine." Tottering and shaking in all his giant frame, he stumbled slowly from the room.

"God help us!" said Holmes after a long silence. "Why does fate play such tricks with poor, helpless worms? I never hear of such a case as this that I do not think of Baxter's words, and say, 'there, but for the grace of God, goes Sherlock Holmes.'"

James McCarthy was acquitted at the Assizes on the strength of a number of objections which had been drawn out by Holmes and submitted to the defending counsel. Old Turner lived for seven months after our interview, but he is now dead; and there is every prospect that the son and daughter may come to live happily together in ignorance of the black cloud which rests upon their past.

www.ingramcontent.com/pod-product-compliance
Lightning Source LLC
Chambersburg PA
CBHW050826180626
46814CB00004B/1480